Marris,

AMIAYA ENTERTAINMENT LLC
Presents

thanks again for your

the sequel to

support.

FLOWERS BED

BLACK ROSES

Happy Memorial Day

A novel by
Antoine "INCH" Thomas

Antoine "Inch" Thomas

410.

D1070305

Copyright © 2007 by Antoine Thomas

Published by Amiaya Entertainment, LLC
Cover design by: www.MarionDesigns.com
Printed in the United States of America

ISBN#: 978-0-9777544-8-0
Library of Congress control number:
1. Urban – Fiction. 2. Drama – fiction. 3. Bronx – fiction.

"Antoine "Inch" Thomas is an Amazing Story Teller and a brilliant book writer. Black Roses is definitely worth the wait."
—Vito G- Author of *Ill-Na- Na*

"Antoine "Inch" Thomas has delivered a riveting street scorcher. Up- Ending traditional lit, through the eye of its main character, Black Rose."
—Bernard "Talal" Sullivan- Screenwrite & author of the Hoodspense Novel *Kith & Kin*

"Inch has done it again. He's penned another raw epic that even surpasses Flower's Bed. If you liked how raw Flower's Bed was, then you'll love the sequel, Black Roses."
—Charles Threat- Author of *Window Shopper*

"Antoine "Inch" Thomas makes you experience the streets and adversity through the heart of his characters."
—Donald "110%" Capria- SRL Films Screenwriter/ Producer of *Valhalla* and *Central Park*

"Antoine "Inch" Thomas does it again, The Sequel to *Flower's Bed* was Worth the weight."
—T. Coleman Author of *Mother May I*

"Antoine, you never cease to amaze me with your talent. I love the way you hold me down from beginning to end and how I wasn't able to put down *Black Roses*. You'll always be my #1 author forever."
—Tania L. Nunez- Thomas Ceo-Amiaya Entertainment

"Mr. Antoine "Inch" Thomas is an astonishing novelist. He's amazed readers once again with *Flower's Bed Pt. II. Black Roses* is a must read."
—Travis "Unique" Stevens CEO-
Sharpvision Productions, LLC

"Inch is literally redefining Urban Fiction with this thorough depiction of the Game as we know it. *Flower's Bed, The Sequel, Black Roses*, is the truth, manifested in the form of a book! Most definitely… Gangsta!"
—Micheal "Mikeyraw" Whitby Author of *All or Nothing*.

"Damn! Another hot book by the company that took over the hood. Inch is a beast when it comes to making his pen bleed! I really enjoyed *Black Roses*."
—Vincent "V.I." Warren Best selling Author of *Hoe-Zetta*

Acknowledgements

Everybody who copped part one. Thank you, thank you, thank you, thank you. Without you guys there would be no me. Y'all supported me from day one. Y'all looked out with *No Regrets, Unwilling To Suffer* and the love was totally overwhelming with the *Gangsta Sh!t* series. I also want to say thank you for supporting Amiaya Entertainment as a whole because we really appreciate it. Ladies. Sisters. Mothers, daughters, nieces and aunts. Hoodrats, hoochies, babymothers. I can't overstress it enough. You women are the Queens of this earth, and you should always be treated as such.

In Loving Memory
of
Raymond "Big Ray" Simmons

1974-2006

In loving memory of Sean Bell, who was gunned down on the eve of his wedding day, November 25, 2006, in a hail of 50 shots fired by New York City Police Officers. Sean was 23 years old and is survived by his fianceé Nicole Paultre-Bell and their beautiful daughters, Jada and Jordyn.

We Need Justice!

Dedication

Tania, I do everything for everybody else.
But this one's for you, ma.

Prologue

FLASHBACK   PART ONE   9 YEAR OLD FLOWER

"Mom! Mom! Mom! Hurry up! We're going to be late!" Flower exclaimed. She had just turned nine years old and couldn't wait to attend her birthday party. At her Bronx apartment in Claremont Houses on 169th street between Washington and Park Avenues, Flower was clad in a bright yellow flower printed Summer dress. She was jumping up and down, happy and excited about the approaching festivities set for the evening.

Unbeknownst to this young angel, in a few hours, her life would take a drastic turn and never again would things be the same.

"Girl, I'm walking you into that skating rink and once I know that you're safe and that your cake has arrived, I'm off to work." Mrs. Melinda, Flower's mom, was dressed in Gap khaki shorts and a white t-shirt with the *Just Say No!* slogan printed on the front of it.

"Is daddy going to be there?" Asked Flower. She danced circles around her mom displaying a smile that personified her preciousness and innocence.

"Of course your father's going to be there, honey. He

never misses any of your birthday parties." Mrs. Melinda assured.

SHOWTIME

It took twenty minutes for Mrs. Melinda to drive Flower and Flower's best friend Rosalyn to the Skate Key skating rink on White Plains Road and Allerton Avenue.

"It's *my* birthday, mister! I'm nine years old now." Flower sang to the security guard at the door of the establishment. She was in bunny hop mode again.

"You are? Happy Birthday young lady." The muscular, heavily tattoo'd bouncer knelt down to make himself the same height as Flower.

Smiling and forever modeling her pearl whites, Flower bashfully rocked side to side and said, "Thank you."

When the children entered the party that had already begun, it went into overdrive. The fiesta started at 7pm and ended about an hour before midnight. Flower pinned the tail on the donkey, earning her a black talking dollbaby equipped with a pacifier, a bib, a full bottle of fake milk and a reusable diaper. She also bobbed the most apples, even though she cheated and used her hands most of the time. With all of the cake she had eaten, Flower wondered if she'd have any room to stomach the candy she received in her gift basket.

After having a fun filled evening, Raymond, Flower's dad, drove the youngsters home in his Alfa Romeo Milano. Rosalyn was dropped off, and once the two of them were alone, Raymond put his scheme into effect.

The Afterparty

"Flower! Flower!" Raymond yelled.

"Yes daddy." Flower barely moved. Her animated video tape had put her into a momentary trance.

"Come here! Come to daddy."

"Okay." Flower answered. She loved her father and always obeyed his guidance. She was into her Barney movie at the moment and didn't really want to abandon her show but did so anyway. "Where are you, daddy? I'm coming." Flower stood up and ran into her mom and dad's bedroom.

"I'm in your room, Flower."

"Yea! Yea! Daddy's gonna tuck me in!" She exclaimed. Flower got to her room and noticed Raymond in her bed underneath her blanket.

Flower placed her hands at her hips, stuck out her lip and pretended to be upset. This is how she would act when she played house with her dolls and needed to lay her smack down. "What are you doing, daddy? You know you're too big to be in my bed."

"Yeah, I know, but daddy loves Flower's bed. Now come here and get under the covers with daddy." Raymond was tapping the bed, encouraging his daughter to come and lay beside him.

Intuition is the power or faculty of knowing things without conscious reasoning and it only comes from the man above. Flower's aura shifted to uncomfortable mode because she was sensing that something was very strange. "Daddy." She said dropping her hands from her waist.

"Come on," called Raymond. He was waving for her to approach him a little bit closer.

"Okay". Flower complied. She climbed into the bed with her father, hid herself under the quilt and peeked over at her hero.

"Flower, you know you can't go night-night with your dress on. Take it off and lay it on the chair."

"Okay, daddy." Flower climbed back out of the bed, pulled her dress slowly over her twists and barrettes, covered her tiny chest and slipped back under the covers.

She was giggling because she was cold and it seemed like the right thing to do to curb the awkward feeling she was currently experiencing.

"Daddy." Called Flower innocently.

· "Huh, "

"Are you going to read to me?" She asked him. Flower was a princess, a rare coin, a jewel, someone you dealt with on the gentlest of levels. Raymond was numb, though. He didn't give a fuck.

So he replied, "No honey, daddy has something special for you tonight that's better than reading."

"Better than reading!" returned Flower excitedly. "What is it? Is it a new doll baby?" Flower was covering her eyes with her small hands, hoping to be surprised with a toy.

"Nope. I have something better, but you have to promise me that you won't tell mommy, okay? You promise?" he said, looking at her.

Flower was still smiling. "Yes daddy, I promise. I cross my heart and hope to die that I won't tell."

Just then, Raymond flung the covers off of himself revealing his swollen manhood.

"Nooooooo!!!"

· · ·

FAST FORWARD   SIX YEARS LATER

Flower was 15 years old and still experiencing terrible nightmares. A year prior, the bad dreams only consisted of images of Raymond abusing her. Every evening when she'd close her eyes, horrible things would take place inside her head. She'd constantly relive every detail of every sexual encounter that would occur between her and her biological father. Unfortunately, for Raymond, he'd been tragically killed almost a year ago in a convenience store robbery/shooting near Gunhill Road. Since then, the nightmares doubled. The compounded images of terror drove Flower to a heightened sense of promiscuity.

She slept with several guys in her neighborhood, and even had daring trysts at school. Then she met a guy named J.R. who brought her to an exclusive strip club in Manhattan called the *V.I.P.* where Flower mastered the art of pole dancing.

"Aye, youngin'," Cherry called out to Flower. Flower was scantily clad in a red thong and matching push up bra. The ladies were in a dressing room in the basement of the establishment freshening up and everybody were in thongs, topless and some were fully nude.

"Yeah, what's up?" Flower replied. She had her arms folded across her chest and she didn't display her beautiful smile.

"You new here?"

"Yup."

"Do you know what you're doing?'

Flower's arms unfolded and found their way to her hips. Cherry's eyes followed Flower's hands and recognized her defensive posture. To ease the tension, she said, "It ain't shit to wiggle your waist and shake your little ass baby girl, you just have to know how to tease."

Cherry continued when a light went off signaling that the stage show was about to begin. "Let's go y'all." She said to all of the girls. To Flower she said, "Aye, youngin', what's your name?"

"Flower."

"Flower? Is that your stage name?"

"No, that's my real name."

"You need a stage name, girl. Have some clown hunting you down and finding out where you live, using your name. Let me see," Cherry spoke as she thought about a good stage handle for Flower. "Angel," She blurted out. "Yeah, Angel."

"Why you call her Angel?" Asked Cinnamon. Cinnamon and Cherry were best friends and had a unique history between the two of them. Both girls had been raped, but what made their situation different, was that they had been assaulted, together, laying side by side. And since then, they've supported one another and stayed attached to each other through sickness and in health and vowed to continue doing so until one or both of them were laid to rest.

Cherry looked at her homegirl, smiled and said, "'Cause, look at her, she's perfect. She ain't no hoodrat, she ain't got no stretch marks, she got a nice fat ass, apple shaped, a nice chest, a gorgeous face and beautiful natural hair. Ain't shit wrong with her. She has to be an angel."

"Keep it, girl." Said Mt. Everchest, brushing past them. Mt Everchest was another girl who danced at the club.

"Let's go y'all," yelled Cherry.

"Come on," Cinnamon cheered.

As all the girls rushed upstairs with Flower on their trail, to herself she thought, *If Only They Knew.*

Flower danced at the V.I.P for almost a year until she

came across a guy named Shawn who caused a change to happen within her life once again, this time for the better.

O'l boy wined her, dined her, treated her like a lady, told her she was beautiful, that she was indeed special, and did other amazing things with her that she thought only happened to lucky ladies. Flower had been raped, violated, stripped of her innocence and tormented since she was nine years old. How could *she* be lucky? How could something like being treated like a human being be happening to *her*? People like Shawn didn't exist in her world, but by the grace of God, Shawn *did* exist. He was real and he was falling head over heels for this fifteen year old princess and victim of a sick father.

Flower's time of living on the edge had finally come to an abrupt end when Shawn asked her to move out to Pennsylvania with him to share the goodness that God gave him, together, as a couple. Flower gladly accepted and the two lovebirds relocated 3 hours west of New York City in a suburb of Reading, Pennsylvania.

In a utopian world, a world of imagination, a world of perfection and paradise, life would seem ideal, and the world would be a land of milk and honey. Unfortunately, that world doesn't exist. In real life, we face problems, struggles, hardships, uncomfortability and sometimes things happen that cause us to lose a little faith. On a warm Summer day, about two years after Flower and Shawn decided to live like Romeo and Juliet, disaster struck, in a way that no one would have ever thought.

"Shawn, I think we should drive up to see my mom. I mean, ever since I've gotten my life together, all I've been able to do is share the happiness of my success through photographs and over the telephone. Rosalyn even stopped coming to visit. She's probably spending all of her time getting to know her new boyfriend," Flower explained.

Shawn was leaning over, tying his shoes. "Oh yeah, I forgot she broke up with your arch enemy. What was his name, Raheem or something, right?"

"Yeah, I never did like his fat ass. He always thought he was a hard rock and a thug." Flower remembered, crossing her arms.

"So are you ready to go up to the City today?" Asked Shawn.

"Hell yeah, let me grab my keys and my purse," Flower got up off the bed and walked over to their closet.

"I gots to hit up the Big Apple with my shines on. A nigga can't be a baller without the jewels hanging in New York. And Flower, you can wear my big chain with the big circle medallion on it." He shouted.

"Alright, I'll be ready in one second. Let me grab my jacket just in case it gets chilly up there tonight."

"Don't forget my chain!"

"I'm not going to forget your chain, Shawn!"

NEW YORK CITY, LATER THAT EVENING

Two unidentified males walked over to Shawn's Toyota Supra as Flower was about to leave a message on her mother's voice mail.

Beeeeep!

"Hello mom, it's me."

Before Flower could finish her message, both men were on either side of the vehicle with their guns pointed into the car.

Click! Click!

"Listen here playa, let me hold that!" Shouted one of the intruders pointing his gun back and forth at the car and at Shawn's face. The other cat had his gun pointed at Flower's upper chest.

"You won't be needing these keys, that watch, that bracelet, that chain, those rings and that bulge in your pocket! Homie, get that bitch out of the car while I strip this faggot. I want to see his bama ass hit that corner and act like he's Jesse Owens!"

When Shawn went to press the power button to cease the vibrating of his ringing cell phone, the last thing either of them heard was, "THIS NIGGA GOT A GUN!"

Then the shots rang out...

Flower came to in Bronx Lebanon Hospital with a gunshot bruise to the chest, courtesy of the bullet being stopped by the big medallion she was wearing, and an entry to her right shoulder. Shawn was struck five times, twice in the head, once in the stomach, and in both arms. He lay still, in a coma, while Flower recovered, regained her strength and sought out revenge on the perps who tried to kill her and her boyfriend.

"Shawn." She said softly during one of her regular visits to her unconscious better half, "I love you more than anything in this world. We've been through so much together and I don't know how I'm going to manage if you leave me alone in this crazy world. You are my right hand and I am your left. When you and I first met, I thought that I wasn't good enough for you. I was this loose, promiscuous little tramp doing anything for nothing. You showed me the way Shawn. You taught me how to respect myself and how to be a woman. You were that shoulder for me to lean on and I won't ever give up on you. I will stay by your side until we're both kicking up daisy's. They tried to shut us down when they robbed us, but we were superhero's that wouldn't die. So listen here, Superman, Superwoman pulled through. I know you will too." By the end of her one way conversation, tears had attached themselves to Flower's cheeks.

In her pursuit of happiness, Flower had caught a bad break, then, a good one soon followed.

"So what brings you back this way?" Mt. Everchest asked Flower in her joyful spirited voice.

"I need a favor." Flower had told her.

"So what, are you trying to hook me up?"

"No, Eve, I just need to place his ass in a situation where I can frame him."

"And you need E-V-E to help you pull it off?" Mt. Everchest showed Flower a smirk as she folded her arms.

"Sort of. You see, he won't come near me anymore because he knows what he did to me almost hit my heart. But God put something there to protect me."

"So what do you need me to do?" Flower was one of the few friends that Mt. Everchest had. If Flower needed help, then Eve would be her support.

Flower smiled, "Let's walk up to the bar."

PAYBACK

Mt. Everchest managed to lure Omar and Raheem, the two assailants who tried to off Flower and Shawn, back to a motel so that Flower could handle her business. Flower waited until Mt. Everchest was out of sight before she entered the room.

"Yo, that bitch is teasing us. I'm going to fuck her in the ass all night for trying to fuck with my emotions." Omar was tied to the bed, adjacent his partner, Raheem, who was tied to the other bed that lay right beside one another.

"Shut the fuck up you fuckin' peon!" Flower cursed as she shut the door behind her. She held the 9mm that she found at J.R.'s apartment a few years prior, with both hands, the way she was taught to do at the gun range. "Faggots, you thought I wouldn't come back for you two! Laugh now, muthafuckas!"

"Please don't kill me." Raheem begged after seeing his crimey get hit up a couple of times right next to him by the crazy broad with the gun in her hands.

"It's over Raheem."

"Wait! I'll get you your jewelry." He said trying to buy some time.

"Fuck that jewelry, and fuck you too!" Flower then aimed and hit Raheem five times in his neck and torso before landing a fatal shot to his face. She then turned the gun back on Omar and gave him six more sleeping pills to the chest. *Boom! Boom! Boom! Boom! Boom! Boom!*

"That's what happens when you punish a bitch and don't kill her." Then she exited the motel making a safe and unnoticed getaway.

SIX MONTHS LATER

Shawn woke up from his coma and when he was eventually able to speak, he shared with Flower a special dream that he remembered having.

"You know, when I was in that coma, I knew I was in bed. Somebody's bed. In the dream, I would toss and turn and I'd wake up and see this silhouette lying next to me. But when I'd reach for it, it was too far for me to touch so I would lay there and wonder, *Whose bed am I in?* Then, I guess right before I began to regain consciousness, the silhouette began to take shape. I got nervous at first, but then I relaxed when I realized that the shape of the silhouette belonged to the most important person in the world to me. It was you Flower. That silhouette was you all along. And only then was I able to sleep comfortable in my dream because I knew where I was. I was in Flower's Bed!"

Chapter One

"Shawn! Shawn! Are you home, boo!?" Flower called out as she entered her home through a side entrance. When her husband didn't respond, she turned around, aimed her keychain at her CLK and re-engaged the alarm system. *Boop! Bop!* Flower's Benz was sitting on 24-inch floaters. The coupe's exterior was crimson maroon which she called *Cherry Coke* while the vehicle's guts were a peanut butter brown. "I know he's here because I can hear that dag on game." Flower was speaking in a low tone as she quietly searched for her husband.

"Pass the ball, stupid. Pass it. Okay, okay! Wade…in your face! Watch the dribble. Now I'ma take it to the hoop on yo' ass." Shawn was playing NBA 2K7 featuring Jay-Z on his X-Box in the basement of their home. "Come on Wallace, come on!" he yelled. Shawn was pressing the buttons on the joystick aggressively, trying to bring his player up the court without losing possession of the rock. Once under the rim, Shawn pressed the *jump* button, hit the *up* button two times, and then he pressed the *forward* button three quick times. Ben Wallace of the Detroit Pistons scored the final shot of the game with a slam dunk making the final score 81-80, Detroit over Miami.

"Are you happy that your team has finally beat us?" Flower chirped from the sideline. She was standing in the doorway that led to the basement, with one hand on her hip while her other hand clutched her Louis Vuitton purse.

Shawn turned around and said, "Flower, you know we always bust y'all's ass." He smiled, remembering the last time him and his wife played against one another. Flower's favorite team was the Miami heat and every time they went up against one another, Shawn would pick Detroit. The last time the couple went at it, Shawn made a $50 bet that he'd beat Flower and Miami by a dub. The final score was Miami 99, Detroit 123. The two lovebirds ended up squashing their bet in the bedroom.

"Nah, uh, y'all only beat us when it's me against you, and you know that I'm not too familiar with all of them fancy moves they be doing." Flower sat on the arm of the sofa and gently rubbed Shawn on the nape of his neck. It was an affectionate gesture that she'd practiced on many occasions.

Shawn turned his attention to the component and ejected the disk. Then he faced his wife again, "You're right, but do know this," he said, grabbing Flower by her chin and kindly positioning her face so that they were eye to eye with one another. He then leaned in close to his significant other, looked deeply into her eyes and said, "We just won the championship. And as a champ, I think we should celebrate." Shawn grabbed Flower by her waist, pulled her down onto the sofa with him and shoved his tongue deep down her throat.

"Horny, aren't we?" Flower mumbled with Shawn's tongue tangled up with hers.

Within minutes, the two lovebirds were naked, with

Shawn sliding in and out of Flower from the back. Flower's knees were sunk into the pillows, while she rested her elbows on the upper part of the couch.

"Talk that shit to me, baby," Flower whispered seductively, "you know I love it when you kick that gangsta shit." Flower had her head turned sideways trying to look at her husband as his face contorted from the beautiful feeling of her inner walls.

Shawn had a steady rhythm. "You like it, boo? Huh, ma? You like how the magic stick beat that pussy up?" Shawn was gritting his teeth and occasionally knawing down on his bottom lip. "You like this dick, right? This your dick, ma, all yours." He stood up on the sofa, grabbed Flower underneath her chin and forced her lips to his while he continued to pound away.

Flower repositioned her head and noticed her reflection in the mirror. When she spotted her husband's face and recognized *that look*, she went all out and put her back into it. Flower contracted the muscles in her coochie so that her pussy tightened up and squeezed Shawn's penis. She arched her back which allowed Shawn to reach another sensitive spot in her love tunnel and began to speak back to her husband. "Right there, honey, that's it, that's the spot. Faster, fuck me faster, Shawn." She begged in between moans.

Shawn increased his speed by only a notch.

"Harder Shawn, give it to me! You know how your baby girl likes it."

Shawn pumped harder, making the slapping sound increase as his pelvis smacked into Flower's butt cheeks.

"Deeper, babe. Give me everything you got, oh!" Flower was having her moment. Her head was moving like a roller coaster at an amusement park. Everytime Shawn's rod would slide in, to its hilt, Flower's head would lift up and rotate either way. When Shawn would pull out, readying himself for another stroke, Flower would exhale, lower her head and rotate it in the opposite direction.

Shawn increased his strokes. His testicles were slapping up against Flower's clit and it was driving her crazy.

Flower began trembling. She suddenly stopped humping back.

Shawn knew she was cumming. He spread his wife's ass cheeks as far as he could, looked down at himself reappear and vanish inside of his spouse's love nest, and rotated his waist. He continued drilling, and when he felt himself beginning to cum, he slammed his rod up into Flower as far as he could and held her like a vice grip. "Aaahh!" Shawn released some energy and collapsed on top of his woman.

"Shawn?" Flower spoke exhaustedly. She sighed and rested her head on the backrest of the sofa.

"Hmmm." He too was out of it. He erected his torso and allowed his head to lean back.

"What are you doing?" Flower was smiling now.

"Nothing." Shawn chuckled but continued doing what he was doing.

"Yes you are, I can feel it." Flower was feeling Shawn contract his dick muscles as his penis remained inside of her.

"Chill, I'm trying to empty it all out. You never know, one of them bad boys might penetrate the sperm police down there that you call birth control."

Flower began humping her husband until his love stick became soft and slid out. "Shawn, we talked about this. You know I'm on a mission right now." She smiled faintly.

Shawn repositioned himself and his wife and had Flower

sitting on his lap, cowgirl style. "I know honey, I know. I just love you so much and I can't wait until we start our own family." Shawn had his puppy dog face on.

"I know Shawn, I want children just as bad as you do but if we start now, I'll never finish the 'Heart Foundation Tour.' Those women need me out there. Especially the young ones, they depend on me." Flower whined. Going out and talking to women in need gave Flower purpose. No longer did she dedicate herself to the struggle just because.

Shawn leaned into his wife and kissed her. "Promise me something, Flower. Promise me that as soon as this tour is over, we'll start working on our family." Just the thought of Flower being pregnant caused Shawn's soldier to stand back at attention. He stared at her as a smile crept onto his handsome face.

Flower felt Shawn's little man rise for the occasion. She lifted her butt a little bit, eased back down onto her baby's shaft and whispered, "I promise. In the meantime, let's practice." She smiled and the humping resumed right where it left off.

• • •

"Flower! Flower!" Shawn was lying on their bed watching BET. He had on a pair of blue Sean John jeans and a white T-shirt.

"Shawn, were you calling me?" Flower turned off her blow dryer and stared awkwardly into the air.

"Yeah."

"What's up honey?" she bellowed.

"I think I heard the mailman."

"So why you ain't check the mailbox?" Flower was in the kitchen watching *The Young And The Restless*.

"Because I'm upstairs. Aye, Flower!?"

"Yeah," Flower got from under the blow dryer and headed for the front door to check the mailbox.

"Did you see Beyonce's new video?"

"Tell me Shawn, what is it about this *Beyonce video* that has you so excited?" She rolled her eyes and paused before opening the door.

Shawn thought that he got caught mind-cheating so he choked up. "What?"

"Shawn, you heard me." Flower grabbed the mail from the mailbox, looked up into the sky, noticed that it seemed like it was going to be a nice day, and then closed the door behind her.

"I just wanted to know if you saw that coat that Jay-Z had on." Shawn was lying and Flower knew it. She didn't care though because she knew where her man's heart was at.

"Yeah whatever," She yelled and pranced back into the kitchen.

"Anything in there for me?"

"I'm still looking, Shawn. Yeah, your phone and pager bills came." She yelled.

"What about the rent? Did our rent money come in yet from the brownstones?" He asked.

"Honey, you know I got that under control."

"Yeah ah-ight!"

"Yeah, I know I'm right." She wiggled her neck.

Flower flipped through her mail and noticed a piece that was marked *urgent*.

I wonder who this is from? She thought to herself. The letter had been post dated out of New York City. Flower opened it up, unfolded the paper and read the letter to herself.

Dear Mrs. Flower Moore,
Hello and how are you doing? Don't be startled that I wrote to you at your home. I mean no harm, really. I looked you up and found your information in the phone book. You're probably wondering what this is all about, right? Like what is this letter in reference to. Well, I've been molested myself. But the difference is, with me, I'm 13 and it's still happening. I didn't want to write to the 'Heart Foundation' because I knew you were still on tour. I have your itinerary. I took a chance writing you at your home because I know you just spoke at the Civic Center in West Philly, and I figured that you might stop by your home since you were in the area (I hope I got lucky-LOL).

Anyway, I've actually been to a few of your venues. I listened to you in Richmond, Virginia. Great speech. You spoke about abuse in the military. That was a wonderful topic!

The seminar at the MCI Center in Northwest, D.C. was touching as well because you spoke about the increase in child molestation by a friend or family member of the same sex. Excellent subject!

At the Baltimore Convention Center in central downtown Baltimore, I'll never forget it. You had on a black leather Prada skirt that was so hot. You had on a beige leather Prada top under a 3¼ beige Fendi coat sweater with a hood attached to it. I also remember it being cold that evening. The Roberto Cavalli boots you had on were the bomb. Beige with black stitching. You were dressed so conservative but yet so sexy. Girl, enough about your wardrobe. Anyway, you mentioned something about drug abuse. You noted that in Baltimore, Maryland, there was an extremely high percentage of drug abusers in their urban community. You said that many of those drug abusers were kids. You explained how *many of those kids and young teenagers turn to a life of drug usage due to trauma that occur in the household. How by being abused as a toddler, young child or teen, that that can possibly lead those kids to abusing. Flower, you always seem to know what to say.*

So I guess New Jersey is next. You'll be speaking in Newark first, and the following day you'll be in East Orange. You'll then make your way to a community center in Livingston, one in Plainview and then you'll be closing out in Jersey City. I can't wait to see you at each event.

You wonder why I would write you something like this, acknowledge the fact that I'm being abused, allow it to continue and not do anything about it? It's simple, Flower, something is wrong here but I don't know what it is. And allowing him to use my body any way that he likes to, makes him feel better. But sometimes I wonder if there is something wrong with me. You're the expert. You tell me. See Ya around.

Sincerely,
Black Roses

"Flower. Flower! Are you okay?" Shawn had walked downstairs, picked up his mail, skimmed through it, and had just finished looking at his pager and cellular phone bills. He didn't want to bother Flower while she read her piece of mail, so he waited. Flower had been finished with her letter for more than two minutes and was staring into the empty space in front of her. "Flow," Shawn nudged her.

Flower jumped, "Huh," she blinked and realized that she had zoned out.

"Are you okay, honey?" Shawn knew that something was wrong and whatever it was, had his wife spooked.

"Shawn, it's happening all over again." She looked at him.

"What's happening all over again, Flow?" Shawn had his hands on Flower's shoulders. His eyes were darting back and forth as he tried to read his wife's mind by looking at her face.

"The pain. Raymond, my father!" her eyes started to water, and her bottom lip trembled.

"What, wha, what do you mean?" Shawn was lost and confused.

"I have to help her." A tear dropped from Flower's left eye.

"Help who honey? Who's she?" Shawn was getting desperate, he had to get to the bottom of this. Flower looked like she was about to have a nervous breakdown and it scared Shawn.

"Her." Flower passed Shawn the letter, opened her floodgates, and ran up stairs.

He read the letter, and after a second time, sat down on a chair at his dining room table. He looked towards the ceiling, sighed and said, "God, please help us."

Chapter Two

"Brothers and sisters of the Newark community, I thank you all for coming out to support this cause. But before I leave," Flower paused to scan the crowd of approximately 2,500 people. "If any one of you would like to speak with me personally, I'll be over at the 'Flower Stand' in just a moment." The Flower Stand was a private booth which Flower created so she could have intimate conversations with anyone who wanted to share their personal situations with her.

Before Flower left the podium, amongst the applause, she tried her best to see if any of the young ladies stood out in any sort of way, indicating that they were the *Black Rose* character. No one seemed out of the ordinary so Flower smiled and left the stage waving at everyone. On the way out, Flower hugged and kissed people she knew, and thanked and encouraged those she didn't.

"That Flower sure gets me worked up, Rose." Said Mr. Herman Purvis, Rose's father.

"Who you telling?" Rose responded sarcastically. Rose was laying at the edge of the bed. Herman noticed Rose's eyes when Rose answered him. Rose's eyes fluttered, brushing daddy dearest off.

"Don't get smart with me, Rose. Now hurry up and take your clothes off." Herman was lying in the bed of their hotel room stroking himself.

Rose undressed slowly.

"Pass me that KY, Rose. And hurry it up!" Herman pressed.

"Anal sex again, dad?" Rose sighed then Rose's socks found their way to the floor.

Herman jumped up and grabbed Rose by the throat. He said, "You listen here, you little sweet, bitch. If you ever come at me crazy again, I will knock all of your teeth out! Do you hear me!?" Herman said angrily.

Rose couldn't answer. Herman's grip was too tight. He shook Rose, then released Rose, pushing Rose on the bed. Herman said, "Fuck the KY, this time daddy is gonna teach Rose a lesson in behavior. *Wanna be a wiseass 101.*" Herman rubbed his hands together greedily.

Rose wanted to cry at the initial moment of penetration but chose to remain strong. The only way to keep Herman form choking Rose to death was to let Herman have his way. Herman never used a condom on Rose. He said he loved the feeling of having Rose's blood all over his penis. After every assault, Rose had to perform oral sex on Herman until he reached his second climax. Whenever Rose misbehaved, *according to Herman*, Rose's punishment was raw penetration. And when Rose was being a good kid, Rose got dealt with gently.

After Rose swallowed all of Herman's semen, Herman smacked Rose on the head and said, "Get the fuck off of me! Clean yourself up then bring your ass back over here. It's bedtime." Herman wiped himself off with a damp wash-cloth, grabbed the remote control and laid back on the bed.

• • •

"Flower, are we stopping off to get a bite to eat?" asked Big B, Flower's tour bus driver. The group was on the New Jersey turnpike headed to East Orange. Big B was about 6'5", 300 lbs, black as brand new tar, but cool as hell.

"Yeah B, find an Olive Garden, I feel like some pasta. Do we all agree?" Flower asked from the rear of the bus. She was seated on one of the bunks looking through the fan mail she received at the Newark venue. From previous engagements, Flower realized that time *wouldn't* allow her to speak with everyone personally. So for those who didn't get an opportunity to sit with her, a fan mail box was set up to accommodate them. During her travels, *and* her off season, Flower would correspond through letters with everyone who couldn't speak with her face to face.

The group agreed on the pasta just as Flower stumbled upon the letter she was somewhat expecting. It was in a plain white envelope sealed with a sticker of two black roses that said, 'Black Roses' on it. Flower dropped the rest of her mail and aggressively tore open the letter. She pulled it out, unfolded it and began to read it.

It read:

"Dear Mrs. Flower Moore,

It's Black Rose again, I loved you this evening. You looked so cute up there too, with your cute little self. My dad said you looked like some shit. He also told me to tell you, 'and these are his words, not mine', but he wanted me to tell you that you're a stinking fucking bitch! Flower, I would never say anything like that about you. Again, I loved your outfit. What were those shoes, snake? Gator? Ostrich? Gurl, they were the bomb. And those silk pants were so form fitting, boo, I almost peed my pants. Hold on, here come my dad. I'm supposed to be sending you hate mail, so bare with me. Flower, you are a slimy, grimey, nasty ass bitch. You talk about all of this abuse shit and all this shit about, you once thought you were a whore, bitch, you are a whore.

We cool, he left. He went to get me a John. Did I tell you that that's how we survive and pay for our travel expenses? Yup, daddy sells me to nasty old men. Mostly white guys. But I only get to perform oral on them or mutual masturbation. Daddy says he's the only one fit to fuck me. Weird, isn't it? I wish I could tell daddy that. He'd kill me though.

Anyway, Flower, we'll be seeing you in East Orange. Don't worry about trying to find out who we are. Daddy makes it almost impossible for anyone to figure out who and where we are. Always remember Flower, I love you. I love your strength and I envy your courage. I wish I were you sometimes. I really do. If I were you, daddy would be somewhere else and I'd be free. So until next time, I'll be wondering if I'm the crazy one. You're the expert, so you tell me. See ya around.

Sincerely,
Black Roses"

"Flower! Are you coming?" Keith checked. Keith was Flower's road manager. He was about 5'9", 180lbs, brown skinned with a short haircut.

Flower snapped out of her trance. "Are they seating us yet?" She asked. She tucked the letter away in her purse and stood up. It's where she had the other one.

"We should have our seats by the time you're ready. Are you ready?" Keith noticed the dismal look on Flower's face when he tried to get her attention.

"Keith, hold up for a minute." Flower retrieved the letters from her purse. She handed them both to him. "Look."

In the middle of him reading the first note from Rose, Big B called out to them, "Aye Flow, Keith, y'all coming or what?" Big B put his hands up for a quick moment as if to say *What up!?*

Flower stepped halfway off the bus and said, "We'll be there in a minute. Just make sure you save us some of the appetizers."

When Keith finished the second letter, he looked over at Flower and said, "Flow, this is crazy."

"I know." She nodded.

"When did you get these?" he asked, holding a letter in each of his hands. He looked at both pieces of paper then brought his gaze back to Flower.

"I received one at home yesterday, the other one, I got today." She looked at Keith like she had no idea of what to do.

"Do you want to call the police and hire security Flow, cause I'll,"

Flower cut him off with a wave and a chuckle, "No security Keith. I ain't no dag on rapper. Besides," she smiled. "that ain't my style." Keith could tell that her smile was simply a replacement for the tears that she was holding back. Everybody knew about Flower. It was even said that a book had been written loosely about her.

"So what do you suggest we do, Flow?" Keith wanted to take some action. He loved Flower like a little sister and her husband Shawn was his first cousin. He promised Shawn that he'd take very good care of her while they were on the road.

"Relax Keith. Let's just play it by ear for now. I don't even know who these people are, for Christ sakes. I mean Rose could be white, black, Spanish," Flower had the letters in her hand waving her arm in the air for emphasis.

"A serial killer." Keith chimed in.

"I don't think it's that deep, Keith. As a matter of fact, I was thinking," She put the letters back in her purse.

"Uh oh, don't do anything stupid, Flower." Keith had his hand close to Flower's face waving his index finger side to side.

"I'm not. Once we get inside, I'll inform the gang on what's going on and I'll also share with y'all what I have in mind." She smiled.

"Whatever it is Flow, I know you, so I know it's gonna be something crazy."

"It won't be, you'll see." She modeled off her pearlies again.

The duo left the tour bus and joined their hungry friends inside of the Italian restaurant.

• • •

Ring…Ring…Ring

"Hello, you reached the *Moore* residence. If you're calling for," Shawn picked up.

"Hello, hello." He called into the receiver.

"Messing around with that game again, ain't cha?" Flower guessed happily. There was a smile plastered across Flower's face and Shawn could sense it.

"I was just about to have Lebron dunk on ya boy Carmelo." Shawn was out of breath from running for the phone. He plopped himself down on the living room sofa.

"Stop hating on Carmelo Anthony." Flower told him.

"I ain't hatin', I'm just saying." He looked down at the new BAPE's that he had on his feet.

"You're just saying what?" Flower was blushing from ear to ear because she hadn't spoken to her husband since the night before and hearing his voice always brought a smile to her face.

"That you only like Carmelo because he looks like me."

"You and Carmelo do not look anything alike." She squinted up her face and then smiled.

"We don't?" asked Shawn. He was faking like he was surprised.

"No!" Flower smiled harder, "you look better."

"That's right, don't hate the playa, hate the game."

"Whateva." She waved his statement off and rolled her eyes playfully.

"Nah, what's up with you, honey? How's the tour going?"

"It's cool." Flower thought for a minute on whether or not she should tell her husband about the new letter. Shawn was very overprotective when it came to his wife. With all of the stuff that she had been through, Shawn vowed not to let anything happen to her ever again.

"Guess what?" She said.

"What?"

"Guess?" Flower shook her head slowly and made a face that said, *Use your thinking cap, stupid.*

"The tour is coming to an end?" Shawn was beaming crazy.

"No." His smile turned into a frown.

"You found out that I finally penetrated the sperm police?" He smiled again.

"No, stupid. Those sperm police are like Homeland

Security, they're holding shit *down.*" They both laughed.

"Tell me Flow, I give up."

"Promise me you won't get all jumpy." She asked him. She threw that out there because she knew that Shawn still had that 'hood shit up in him and would go bonkers at the drop of a dime.

"I promise." Shawn got real serious.

"Black Rose sent me another letter."

There was silence between the couple for about 10 seconds before anyone spoke up. Shawn didn't know what to say. He knew how much the 'Heart Foundation' tour meant to Flower and he also knew that she could take care of herself if need be. He just didn't want her to be alone.

"Are you okay?" he asked carefully.

"Yeah, I'm ah-ight. You?" She countered.

"I'm good."

"So how do *you* feel?" She could tell her husband wasn't too cool about the whole stalking thing, so she added, "I'm okay, boo. Keith is here with me. The entire gang. I'm fine. I just think Rose wants me to help her." She figured.

"And you're fine with this?" He was asking her to make sure that *she* was sure.

"It's what I do Shawn. You know me, I live for the drama." She smiled again.

"Okay, but the minute I feel like something is wrong, I'm on the next thing smoking and I'm bringing you home. You understand that!"

"Comprende, husband of mine."

"So what are you doing now?" He fished.

"Well right now everyone is stretching. We just ate and we're about to head out to East Orange. Here comes Keith, you wanna talk to him?" She offered.

"Yeah, lemme holla at him."

"Okay, I love you, Shawn."

"I love you too, Flow."

"Don't worry honey, everything will be okay. Trust me." She said.

"I do. I just love your ass so much." He closed his eyes and thought about the pretty ass smile that she kept on display.

"I know. Now give me some love."

Mmtwa!

Mmtwa, "Love you. Here's Keith." Flower returned the sugar, then handed Keith the phone.

Flower had jumped back on the tour bus, opened up the letter again, and took a seat at her desk. She pinned the letter up next to the first one and just looked at them. "Talk to me, Rose. I know you want this shit to end. Show me your face. Just one time, show me your face."

Chapter Three

Ring…Ring…Ring!

"Hello, H.P. here."

"You got the kid?" Asked the John.

"Ready when you are." Herman Purvis replied.

"How much?"

"$500, same as always."

"Whatever I want?"

"Of course not. Oral or mutual masturbation. You know the deal." Herman reminded the customer.

"Well what are you waiting for?"

"Your room number."

"Room 112."

Click!

In The Hotel

"What's a matter, Rose? You don't like what you see?" teased the John.

"I never like what I see. What's pleasure for you, is business for me. So why don't you pull your stuff out and let me get this over with. Besides, isn't your *wife* gonna be expecting you soon?" Rose commented with a sarcastic smirk. Rose had been with this particular John on many occasions and was aware that the old pervert was married.

The John engaged a smirk of his own, then he let out a small chuckle. He sat back in his chair, unzipped his pants and pulled out his penis. "Take off your clothes. I want to see how excited you become once you've tasted the king."

Rose undressed and stood there, using whatever there was available to cover up.

"No need to be ashamed,. You're beautiful, Rose. Come on over here."

Rose approached the John, a white man, early 40's with a trim build.

Rose bent over and sucked on the John until his Johnson became erect.

"Continue," encouraged Mr. Sicko, "Keep sucking until I say stop. When I say, are you ready for the money shot, you stop sucking and you sit your pretty face close enough so that my cum can reach those beautiful lips of yours. Do you understand?" Rose just looked at the dude. After a brief stare down, o'l boy handed Rose five one hundred dollar bills one at a time.

Rose quickly grabbed the money and placed it into the pocket that Herman said was the cash register, Rose's single back pocket.

Herman called that pocket the cash register because he said that one day Rose's ass would be worth a lot of money. But until then, the perverts of society would have to accept what Herman allowed to happen.

Rose performed like a pro and in less than a minute, the John was yelling, "Show me the money! Show me the money!" That was Rose's cue. Rose stopped sucking and pulled on the guy's penis until he erupted. Fortunately for Rose, the John was a light squirter. Rose washed up, got dressed, and left the hotel room. And as always, Herman was right outside waiting.

When Rose entered the vehicle, the first thing Herman said was, "Do you have my money?" Rose replied in the affirmative. Then Herman said, "Now give me a kiss."

As Rose leaned into Herman and began kissing him, someone from across the street was practicing their photography. The photographer accidentally caught shots of Herman and Rose in inappropriate and uncompromising positions but wouldn't find out until after the film had been developed.

"You better not have given him any, either. You know I'm going to check you out when we get home." And with that, Herman threw the car in drive, *Click, Click*, and took off. *Click, Click!*

Rose sat back and sighed. *I can't wait 'til this mothafucka gets tired of me.*

East Orange, New jersey. The Following day

"Ladies and gentlemen, thank you again for coming out and supporting the cause. It's very rare that we can come together and celebrate this liberal point in our lives." Flower was standing at the podium dressed in a denim Baby Phat skirt, matching denim Baby Phat knee high boots and a white blouse. "We must remain strong. We must remain free.

45

We must remain courageous. We must maintain our strength. We must never ever give up and we must certainly never be afraid. When you see trouble approaching, walk away. When you see drama headed your way, turn around. And if you can't get rid of your problem, ask someone for help. Someone will reach out to you. It's up to you to make the first step. Then everything else will follow.

"In a moment I'll be relocating over to the 'Flower Stand'. For those of you who would like an up close and personal, be my guest."

Since reading the two letters, Flower had decided not to dwell on the situation and instead sit back and prepare her speech for the next event. The East Orange event was over, the love the crowd showed was overwhelming and just as Flower was about to get up and head for the tour bus, she spotted a white man and what appeared to be a young Black female racing through the crowd.

Flower frantically pushed and shoved her way through the crowd, "Move, mmph. Excuse me. Aah! Watch out." Trying her best not to lose the duo. As soon as she made it to the parking lot, a grey conversion van sped out of the area possibly taking along with it any chance of an encounter with Rose.

When Flower began walking to the venue, on the ground she found an envelope. It was addressed, *Mrs. Flower Moore*. This time around, the contents of the letter were so far, the most horrific.

Chapter Four

After the long, exhausting tour, Flower found herself cuddled up next to her husband, who was snoring quietly in their king sized bed.

Flower fingered the letter that she promised herself not to show Shawn.

The letter she had received from one of her last venues had caught her totally off guard. Inside the envelope was a bloody condom with a letter inside of it sealed with semen. Flower had at first jumped when she tore open the envelope, startled by what she had found. She quickly regained her composure, found her some latex gloves, removed the scribe from the rubber, opened it and read the single sentence. The letter had obviously not been written by her friend Rose because it read: *In a minute, you and Rose will be two bloody tulips. Get it, two lips.*

Flower had let out a quick scream after she read the kite but caught herself before anyone of her crew could catch on. She tucked the letter, like she had done the two previous ones, and now she laid in her bed, fiddling with the latest installment of the *Black Rose drama*.

Flower closed her eyes for a brief moment when all of a

ANTOINE "INCH" THOMAS

sudden Shawn let out a soft moan. With her eyes extremely heavy and still closed, she nudged Shawn softly with her elbow, hoping that he'd quiet it down. The moan appeared again so Flower opened her eyes and tapped him at the same time. That's when she noticed that it wasn't Shawn doing the moaning, it was what appeared to be a young boy bent over the arm of Flower's recliner chair that she had in her bedroom. The boy had a ball that was attached to two straps, stuffed in his mouth, with his hands tied, extended behind his back. A white man was humping the kid doggie style causing the kid to moan. Flower knew she was dreaming but when she went to nudge Shawn again, his lifeless body fell to the floor.

Flower screamed, assuming that she would suddenly wake up. However, this wasn't a dream. This was far from fantasy land. This shit was real and Flower was now in a fucked up situation. Her husband was lying on the floor, next to their bed, stiff like the dick that the white man was sliding up in the youngin. Shawn had a hole in his head the size of a boiled egg, courtesy of a bullet from the silenced 9mm that the white man had aimed at the child's head whom he was raping right there in Flower's bedroom

"Shit," Flower whispered. She thought about the most recent kite she had received from Rose, *In a minute, you and Rose will be two bloody tulips. Get it, two-lips.* "Rose," she managed to say a little more audibly as she tried to swallow. Flower's throat felt like sand and her hands and feet would not move.

Rose moaned again, hoping that his screams could be heard over the object in his mouth.

Flower shook her head and blinked her eyes. The whole scene was crazy. First of all, Rose was a boy. His limp penis

48

and sagging nutsack proved that much. And, he was black, but had a white man, perhaps the father, perhaps a foster parent, up in him like it was a scene out of a gay, perverted porno tape. Shawn, Flower's husband, her partner, her life, was dead and gone. A slug to the dome piece, and Flower had no idea when, *or* how it went down.

She could have sworn she just closed her eyes for only a moment, a second ago.

She brought her gaze back to Mr. Purvis, who now had his 9mm pointed at her. He smiled. Then he looked over at Flower's nightstand. When she followed his eyes she locked in on the glass of Kool Aid that she thought Shawn had placed up there for him to drink. Shawn always kept some fluids laying around in case he got thirsty after a love session or whenever he woke up in the middle of the night. Flower had taken a few sips of the substance herself when the room was dark. Now that it was illuminated by the visual that appeared on the 62" plasma that sat adjacent to the bed, Flower noticed the skull and bones logo that was applied to the side of the cup. Flower figured that she had been drugged which is why she didn't hear when Herman entered her home. He some how shot and killed her husband while he lay in the bed right next to her and set up the eerie scene that played itself out before her. Dude was probably about to kill her *and* Rose, according to the last letter that she received.

Herman Purvis spoke up, "That's right my darling Flower." He now had his gun pointed at her face. Flower was stuck and in shock. She hadn't moved a finger, blinked nor did she inhale or exhale, and didn't plan to. Herman had shit on smash. "Yeah, everything that you're probably thinking is very fucking true. I adopted Rosevelt when he was three years old, waited until he was ten and fucked him!"

Herman laughed heartily. "I fucked him mentally and, as you can see," he stroked two quick times, "literally." He then released a 50 Cent laugh. "Then you and this Heart Foundation crap started fucking things up. Rosey here started becoming apprehensive toward my advances and I later found out why. He had a tape of you in action, hidden under his pillow that I beat him with until it broke. This crack baby came from one of you black people's neighborhoods and I offered to take good care of him. I raised him like the monkey that he is and fed him my banana every time he got hungry."

Rose was crying softly at first, but now the tears were racing each other. Herman continued, "when I got fed up with your antics, I followed you. I planned, I plotted and now I got your black ass. Now, you and Rosey here will be pushing up daises. Isn't that cute." Herman pulled Rosevelt's head back real hard and stroked him while he spoke through gritted teeth, "Pushing, up, motherfucking, daisies."

Suddenly a red dot appeared on the side of Herman's head. Then a piece of glass popped from Flower's bedroom window and hit the floor. Another red dot appeared on Herman's head, but this one wasn't from the infra red beam that one of the FBI's top of the line sharp shooters had seconds before placed on his head. That second red dot was blood dripping from a hole in Herman's temple.

That's the last thing that Flower remembered before waking up to a room full of people at Reading Medical Center. Big B, Keith, Mrs. Melinda-Flower's mom, Mrs. Berkowitz-Flower's family friend and counselor, and Rosalyn, Flower's closest friend, were all present. Rosalyn also had her 7 year old daughter, Amiaya with her.

Everyone was gathered together talking and comforting Flower. She had been in the recovery unit, from an abundance of psychological and emotional trauma and was due to be released in a few days. For the time being, Flower decided to enjoy her time with her loved ones because she knew when the time came for her to confront Rosevelt, it would be one of her hardest and most emotional times in her young life.

Chapter Five

One Year Later

Flower was tidying up around her apartment, picking up clothing, sweeping, wiping down furniture and mopping the floors, when she came upon Rosevelt sitting in his room. He was alone, perched up on the bed, staring awkwardly at the empty space in front of him. From the position he had taken on the full size Superman comforter that Flower had found in Shawn's closet, she could see a school of tears steadily flowing down his cheeks.

Quietly but careful enough not to startle the young boy, Flower pulled up beside him, eased her arm around his shivering body and embraced him with the right amount of love he needed at that exact moment.

Rosevelt was going through it, consciously reliving one of the terrifying nightmares that haunted him most of his young life.

"Am I ever going to be a normal boy again?" Young Rosevelt asked over his tears. His voice was barely above a whisper and cracked as he spoke.

"You *are* normal, darling. You are not different than anyone else out there." Flower wiped the inner corners of her eyes and lower eyelashes because she too began to cry.

"Why did he hate me so much, Ms. Flower? What did I do so wrong that I had to be punished so severely? Why didn't I just get regular beatings like other kids received?"

Flower thought that Rosevelt was referring to Herman Purvis so she said, "You didn't do anything wrong, chile. Nor did that man hate you. He was just sick. A sicko that didn't know any better. You're a normal, regular kid, Rosevelt, with a lot of love in your heart and you have good people around you now that want to care for you. We're gonna love you like you're supposed to be loved." Rosevelt's head was pressed up against Flower's chin so he felt it when she forced a smile.

She was still holding onto him and had subconsciously began a slow rocking movement. Mrs. Berkowitz had once explained to Flower that cradling a loved one was a rational reflex and a strong sign of comfort and protectiveness. At that moment, Flower was exercising a bit of both.

Rosevelt sniffed back a tear and clarified the direction of his question. "I was talking about God, Ms. Flower. I wanted to know why God doesn't like me. I know my daddy didn't mean to hurt me sometimes, because he would tell me that he was sorry when I cried a lot. He told me he loved me and that he couldn't control himself. And he bought me the X-Men remote control car that I always wanted, too. When I would tell him that I was hungry, he would feed me. He said some kids didn't have any food. And when I was sick, he gave me cough syrup and aspirin for my headaches. We used to see sick kids on TV and he said that I was lucky to have a dad who cared. And one time when he wanted to do it to me,

I told him to wait. Then I said, 'daddy, why do you like to hurt the inside of my body all the time?' He told me that God told him to do it." Flower shook her head, expressing how ashamed she felt of Mr. Purvis. This madman, who was entrusted with this little boy's safety, was telling the kid to be grateful for things that were *supposed* to take place between a parent and a child. Rosevelt felt Flower's tears drip onto his head. He caressed her hand and said, "It wasn't daddy who wanted me to hurt down there," he pointed to his backside, "it was God. Can you tell me what I did to make God angry at me? Huh, mom? Misses Flower, can I call you mommy since I don't have a mommy or a daddy no more?" He leaned up and looked at her. He sniffed again and a tear fell from both of his eyes.

Rosevelt's sweet, innocent, inexperienced words of misunderstanding damn near crumpled Flower. She tried to be strong, but she couldn't help the overwhelming growing emotions she had for young Rose. Flower cried hard for a long time as she maintained her grip on the child. Confused and somewhat scared himself, Rosevelt started crying some more, too. After about twenty minutes of bawling, shrieking and hollering, Flower finally calmed herself *and* Rosevelt, and did her best to help the youngster understand the perplexing, incomprehensible, sad situation.

She said, "Rosevelt, of course you can call me mommy. And I promise I won't let anybody hurt you ever again. Now, as far as Mr. Purvis saying that God wanted him to do those horrible things to you, he was being untruthful. God is good and only loves everyone. You didn't do anything wrong to God or to anybody else for that matter. And God wasn't angry at you, either. My past experiences are what brought us together and I can assure you, that at one time, I thought that God hated me also. I thought that I must have been a bad little girl somewhere down the line and that I too deserved what was happening to me. Ultimately, I thought that it was all my fault. That the pain and suffering that I endured, that I brought it all upon myself."

"You felt like that too?" Rosevelt interrupted. It was surprising and a shock that someone had gone through and felt the same thing that he felt, when he was at his lowest, and could also relate.

"Mm hmm," she confirmed.

"*Was* it your fault?"

"Uh uh." She shook her head. "It wasn't my fault. My father hurt me because he was sick, like Mr. Purvis. Those guys had serious problems going on in their minds that you and I will never understand. We'll never be able to figure them out. We just have to understand and remember that God loves us. That he saved us from that pain, and that we must always be strong or the sickos will defeat us. As we move on we realize that we are special. That God put us through the trials that we overcame, for a reason. I think mine was to save people like you and I. I don't know, but it's what I feel and what I believe." Flower smiled out a tear, caressed Rosevelt's shoulder and kissed him reassuringly on the top of his head. "One day you'll discover your own talents. You'll dig deep into your own soul and reveal a side of you that you never knew existed. You'll take that and you'll work it until you've forgiven Mr. Purvis. Then and only then, will you be able to be free. They say it's a reaction of our trauma. Whatever it is, it'll come. It' always does."

Chapter Six

4 Years Later

Once again back is the incredible, rhyme animal...Stop the presses, I'm back! Cooked Coke that is—-*CRAACK!* "Yo, turn that shit down!" Rosevelt, who opted only to be acknowledged as B.R., by everyone, except Flower and Amiaya, was giving an order to one of his workers.

"Yo, who the fuck is that parked across the street in that Cherokee!" B.R. was in the Bronx, standing in front of his building on 169th Street between Washington and Park Avenues.

"I'ma go see who it is right now." Lil Hahmo stepped up while simultaneously cocking the hammer on his 380.

"Go that way and I'ma go this way," Lil K.I. told his brother, Lil Hahmo. Lil K.I. approached the SUV from its rear while his brother walked directly up on the driver's side window. Lil K.I. unholstered his Ruger and put one in the head, *Click!*

B.R. folded his arms across his chest, discreetly placing his palms on both .45's that he had tucked on opposite hip bones. He had on a pair of white leather Air Max's, some black denim Akademik jeans and a black Lacoste polo button up.

Lil Hahmo, draped in his customary crimson, walked right up on the 4X4, pulled out his .380 and knocked the driver's side window into the lap of an Indian looking dude sitting behind the wheel, "Fuck is you sitting out here scheming on, mafucka! Huh!" Lil Hahmo maintained a safe distance but kept the nozzle of the .380 in sync with Mr. Indian's nose.

Lil K.I. pulled open the passenger side door and caught Mr. Cherokee's sidekick, reaching for some shit that looked like a supersized Desert Eagle. "Duck Hahmo!" Lil K.I. yelled.

It wasn't the first time Lil Hahmo and Lil K.I. had run up on a nigga sitting in his whip plotting on their spot. So Protocol was second nature. Lil Hahmo dropped to the floor and aimed his gun right above the door handle of the truck.

On the opposite side, Lil K.I. let loose, *Bong, Bong, Bong, Bong, Bong!* Killing the passenger where he sat.

Mr. Miyaki tried to climb out of the window on Hahmo's side of the car and as soon as his melon came into view, *Bloom!* Lil Hahmo kicked dude's head into the sunroof of the jeep with a slug from his handgun.

"Come on!" B.R. yelled from his post across the street. "Everybody inside, B.G.!" B.R. turned around and called out to Lil K.I. and Lil Hahmo's other brother, the third triplet. B.G. was sitting on a slab of concrete in front of their building eating sunflower seeds, spitting the shells into a pile in front of him. He was watching the whole scene unfold like it was an episode of *Cops*.

"Yo," B.G. responded calmly.

"Close up shop until Homicide comes through and do

what it is they do. If you see anybody talking to one-time, let me know and we'll introduce them to Amy and Katie if need be." B.R. was referring to his two favorite AK's.

B.G. slid off the concrete monument and entered into the building behind his brothers, who both ran up the same staircase.

"Excuse me," B.G. said to the little girl fighting her way to the front of the vestibule to exit the building.

"Move, nigga!" Amiaya said to B.G. who had just mushed her playfully, and received a kick in the leg for doing so. "Rosevelt!" She yelled out. She looked across the street and frowned at the bloody carnage.

B.R. turned around and almost released one of his jumpoffs until Amiaya's pretty little 12 year old face rolled her eyes at him. "What?!" He said. B.R. spoke in a half angry, half *What do you want?* tone of voice.

"Aunti Flower said she heard some shooting and to bring your black ass upstairs, *now*!" She rolled her eyes. She knew that although Black Rose was crazy and had 169th Street on lock, that whenever Flower called, he would drop everything he was doing and move like his life depended on it.

"Tell her I'll be up there in a minute." B.R. said with his face tightened up.

Amiaya rolled her eyes again and wiggled her neck real hard. Then she sucked her teeth at B.R. and said, "Can I have twenty dollars?" She had her hand extended with the other one on her hip.

B.R. heard the sirens approaching, glanced around again, getting a good look at everyone in eyesight who were outside, then looked down at Amiaya. She stared back up at him without a care in the world so he just brushed right past her.

As he entered the staircase on his way to a stash crib they

had in the building, Amiaya put her nosiness out on display. "I'm telling Flower y'all shot somebody again." And with that, a bell sounded, indicating that the elevator had made it to the lobby. When the conveyor door opened, Rosalyn stepped out and glared at her daughter.

"AMIAYA!" she yelled. Amiaya was used to her mother's hollering because she realized early on that Rosalyn was all bark and no bite. "It's people shooting out here and your silly ass down here being nosy. Get your ass on that elevator and take your butt upstairs!"

Amiaya said, "Dang," and hopped on the ironbox.

"What chu' say to me little woman!? I'll slap your lips off your face and into those buttons if you say something else. SAY SOMETHING ELSE!"

Neighbors on the first floor had begun peeking out of their doors wondering what all of the commotion was about. When the elevator door closed and began carrying its occupants to their designated floor, Amiaya crossed her arms, leaned her weight to one side of her body and sighed real loud.

Rosalyn ignored her daughter and was just happy that Amiaya was safe.

• • •

As soon as B.R. entered the building, the dude that was hiding in the back seat of the Cherokee, kicked Mr. Indian and the passenger out of the vehicle. He closed both doors, sparked the ignition and made a right on Park Avenue, just in time to miss the first squad car bend the corner.

Dude felt his head where a bullet had grazed him and said, "Damn, I'm a kill them Lil Blood niggas. Then I'm gonna kill their boss."

• • •

Upstairs in Flower's apartment

When B.R. slammed the door behind him he yelled, "Ma, what up? You was looking for me? Amiaya told,"

"Hell yeah I was looking for your ass. Somebody was out there shooting, Rosevelt, and I hope you didn't have anything to do with it!" Flower had rollers in her hair and was clad in a pajama pant set and a pair of Prada house shoes.

Ever since the evening that her husband was murdered, and Rosevelt became an official part of Flower's life, things had changed for her. She no longer took pride in her attire, instead, she'd settle for an outfit out of Old Navy or the Gap. She felt there was no reason for the glamour and all the make up anymore since Shawn was gone.

She also worried all day long. B.R. and the street shit that Flower knew he was into had her on pins and balloons. It took about six months, but shortly after the incident, Flower adopted Rosevelt and moved back into her mother's apartment in the Bronx. Mrs. Melinda jumped at the idea when Flower offered her, *her* home, out in Reading, Pennsylvania. Once Melinda felt that Flower was safe and in a comfort zone, especially with Rosalyn and Amiaya around, she packed two suitcases and was on the first Greyhound bouncing west on the Pennsylvania turnpike.

After about a year and a half of mingling with boys his age and getting an up close and personal with a housing project, Rosevelt felt like he was better suited in the streets. He said the experience of his past lead him to where he was, that day, on his last day of school of his sophomore year.

Rosevelt was sitting in front of his apartment reading the article that explained how he and Flower had been saved from a serial rapist. The article said that one day, an off duty homicide detective was taking photos of his young son and daughter in front of a coffee shop which sat across the street from a Holiday Inn hotel, in downtown Reading. The detective said he never remembered seeing anything out of the ordinary that evening but he couldn't deny the images in the photo's that he had developed on his own in the basement of his home. When the first photo of Rosevelt and Herman floated to the surface of the basin, it was extremely clear that a white man was kissing a young black kid in his mouth. The next photo showed an angry white man with his hand plastered against the young boy's face as if the kid was being slapped. The third photo showed the young boy crying. The fourth photo helped them catch, or rather *kill*, a child molester. That photo was a clear shot of Herman's license plate.

A short time later, with enough evidence from the images in the pictures, the FBI secured a search warrant for Mr. Purvis's home. After storming in and combing his apartment from top to bottom, the authorities not only found hundreds of images of different children doing everything under the sun, in their birthday suits, they also found a trail of evidence that led them to Flower's home in Herman's computer.

After reading the article, Rosevelt lowered the newspaper and stared in front of him at the door right across from his. He noticed the feet and nose of his Columbian neighbor's dog, scratching near the floor of the entrance of their apartment. Rosevelt knew the dog was a puppy and pretty much friendly, so he laid down on the floor and began scratching the door from the outside. The puppy seemed to get excited and ran away from the door. A minute later, the puppy returned with his bowl and sat it down near the door then barked twice, *Arf! Arf!*

Rosevelt laughed, and because the neighbors were cool and would always send him to the store, he jumped up without thinking and walked right into their apartment without knocking.

"Hello, anybody home? Mr. Lopez, Mrs. Lopez, it's me, Rosevelt." The dog dashed into a back room and bounced up and down next to a closet door. B.R. followed and assumed the dog's food was kept there, so he opened it up. He couldn't believe his eyes. From the floor to the ceiling was money, wrapped up in plastic, separated in blocks. Beside it were flat slabs of what looked like sheetrock, wrapped individually to mimic small Webster's dictionaries. B.R. knew what time it was, so without messing anything up, he peeled about $120,000 in cash and what eventually totaled twelve kilo's of cocaine. He did it in six trips and hid everything under the bed in his room. Instead of being excited, B.R. played it cool and returned back to his spot on the floor in front of his apartment.

About an hour later, Mr. and Mrs. Lopez returned and entered their apartment with a third party. When his Spanish neighbors stepped over him to get to their apartment, they both spoke, except for their companion. He didn't even acknowledge B.R., which Rosevelt found to be strange since all of the Lopez's friends seemed like nice people.

B.R. waved it off and hoped that he wouldn't soon be questioned by the couple once they found out that their stash had been tampered with.

About ten minutes after the trio entered their apartment, the exit door near the staircase opened up and B.R. was summoned by a wave of a finger to *come here.*

B.R. acknowledged the finger and when he entered the staircase, he noticed about fifty to sixty agents in position to roll on *something*, with their guns drawn.

"Do you live around here?" An agent hidden behind a ski mask asked B.R.

B.R. nodded bashfully and pointed at his door. Then he looked back at the agent.

"Here's what I need for you to do," The agent was nodding his head at B.R., hoping that his gesture would encourage the child's decision. "I need for you to run down those seven flights of stairs as fast as you can. Okay?"

B.R. nodded his head again indicating that he understood the commandment. Then he took off.

About an hour later, the FBI escorted Mr. and Mrs. Lopez out of the building in handcuffs. The third guy never exited; perhaps he was a C.I. and needed to maintain his secret identity. The following day, *The Daily News* and *The CW11 News* ran a story about a big drug bust that went down in a Bronx apartment where authorities seized 190 pounds of cocaine and confiscated $120,000 short of two million in cash.

B.R. smiled and said to himself, "I definitely believe in fate. I watched a tape by Flower Moore, and she eventually became my adoptive mother and legal guardian. I just watched *Scarface* two days ago and bingo, I come off like Tony Montana. All I need now is a mean team and I can turn this building into the Carter."

"Ma, somebody was shooting, but I ain't have nothing to do with it." B.R. said when he snapped back into reality.

Flower pointed her finger at B.R. and gave him a look that said, *keep trying my nerves.*

"I swear ma. It wasn't me." B.R. said it so convincingly

that when he walked up on Flower and kissed her on the cheek, she almost forgot all about the gunshots she heard.

Flower hugged him, then tightened her grip and said, "Rosevelt, you're 18 years old now but I still love you. Those cops got a place for anybody who think they're above the law. I'm telling you, keep playing with these people and they *will* make an example out of your ass."

Knock! Knock! Knock!

Rosalyn and Amiaya knocked on Flower's door and kindly let themselves in without being invited. Rosalyn met up with Flower and walked into the kitchen with her while Amiaya walked up on B.R.

B.R. looked down at her. Amiaya grabbed her hip with a stern face and said, "What!?" She leaned her weight, popped her gum and extended her other hand. "Give me twenty dollars," she said, "or I'm telling Auntie Flower you shot them two men outside."

B.R. peeled off a $20 bill from the knot in his pocket, walked past Amiaya, mushed her down on the couch and exited the apartment.

Chapter Seven

Ever since B.R. crossed paths with that work and those 120,000 reasons to enter the game, life had been treating him real good. He was living like the average rapper pretended to live in their three minute videos.

B.R. was 18 years old and stood at an even six feet. He was naturally muscular with a well defined physique due to the genetics of his unknown parents. Somewhere up the ladder, one of his great grandparents could've been white because B.R. had bright green eyes. The type of eyes that whenever someone saw them for the first time, they'd take a second look and stare for a second just to see if they were actually green.

B.R.'s complexion was walnut brown and he had clear, blemish free skin. He also had soft hair that had many people believe that he was mixed with something exotic. Handsome was an understatement. Depending on how you looked at it, B.R. could've been considered pretty, which is probably why Herman was so inclined to adopt him.

As of his 18th birthday, which had recently passed, B.R. had never been with a woman, and wasn't looking forward to going that route any time soon. He wasn't gay, because he was very much attracted to women. He actually thought Rosalyn was pretty but she was too old for him and was his mother's best friend. Plus he didn't allow anyone to get close to him that he didn't already know. He was satisfied with his small circle of people including Flower, Flower's mom, Mrs. Berkowitz, Rosalyn, Amiaya, and his homies that he ran with, and *ran* niggas off with.

B.R. had a mini mansion tucked away on secluded Esplanade in Mt. Vernon, where he slept at almost every night. The crib was equipped with cameras spread out to cover the entire premises as well as both corners of the block. It was a three-story brick castle that had a four car garage, extra large drive way and a basement that carried everything that the Bally P.T.'s trained with.

It was time to re-up so B.R., dipped in a pair of Catholic school blue, Red Monkey jeans, a white Gino Green Global t-shirt, with large yellow G's covering the top half of the garment, a pair of yellow and white low-cut Air Force 1's and a navy blue World Series New Era Yankee's fitted hat, hopped in a black on black Chrysler 300 sitting on 23 inch spinners and prepared for his trip.

B.R. started the car then turned it back off, half way. The navigation system appeared on the 4" plasma and spoke to the owner of the vehicle. "Please indicate your destination, *Now!*"

"1600 Pennsylvania Avenue." B.R. said calmly. That was the address to the White House. B.R. threw the Chrysler in neutral, applied the emergency brake and watched a secret compartment right next to the gear shifter, open up. He slid his special order .357 automatic off his hip and into the open area for safe keeping. By pressing the cruise control button on the steering wheel, everything popped back into place. The car started up and B.R. drove out onto the street.

As he entered the ramp of the Bronx River Expressway on 233rd Street, Nas continued his one way conversation with the youngster. B.R. felt like the platinum rapper was speaking directly to him when he said, *"Had to hustle hard never give up, that's how I made it/now they're saying that's a clever nigga, nuttin' to play wit'."*

B.R. stayed zoned out as the rest of the CD told its own story. Before he knew it, he was pulling up to a Dominican restaurant on Kingsbridge Road and Sedgwick Avenue in the Bronx.

"Have a seat and Flaco will be with you in one second," An elderly Spanish woman directed B.R. as if it was almost rehearsed as he entered the eatery.

It had taken B.R. a year to form his tight clique and move the twelve kilos that he stole from Mr. Lopez and about four months to secure his current connect. This was the fifth time meeting with Flaco in the last twenty months and every time they dealt with each other, B.R. would purchase two extra kilos and was always charged less each trip.

B.R. started out with a four brick purchase in the beginning, just to make sure that the stuff he was buying was top of the food chain. If it wasn't, the $80,000 loss would easily be compensated by B.R. killing everybody in the restaurant on a crowded busy evening. Fortunately for B.R. the coke was the bomb. The quality of the cocaine was in B.R.'s favor and best interest regarding his safety because Flaco was not only connected, he was a kingpin.

When B.R. first began looking for a connect, he actually connected with Flaco from the gate. Flaco at first declined his advances because B.R. seemed too eager. While being intentionally sent on a search mission, Flaco did a background check on the youngin. Not only did he discover that B.R. had all of his loved ones tucked away in one apartment building, bad move on the hustler's behalf, but B.R. also had zero tolerance for failure.

If you came up short, you worked it off and ended up unemployed. If you stole something, you got beat like a sparring partner with no arms. And if you violated the loyalty code by kicking it with the opposition or the police, your crime was considered to be treason and everybody in your family was killed except you. You were left to deal with the pain and anguish of losing a little brother or sister to a Pitbull mauling or a grandmother to a hit and run. And those stray bullets always had siblings names etched onto the side of their shell casings. Usually the violator would be so consumed with fear that they'd eventually kill themselves.

So after giving B.R. the thumbs up, the first currency/coke exchange went down in this very same restaurant that B.R. was meeting Mr. Poppi Seed at, at that very moment. For over a year and a half now, things were going smoothly and as far as B.R. and Pablo Escobar were concerned, things could only get better.

Flaco appeared from the rear section of the eatery as B.R. scooped the last of the Chic peas he was munching on, into his already full mouth.

"Aye, Pye, wha' 'sup brother." Flaco gave B.R. a handshake and a half hug like if he were used to doing that his whole life. Flaco was young, 28 maybe 29. He looked like Marc Anthony, J-Lo's husband and spoke with almost no broken English. It was more than likely that he was born and raised in New York City because he kept an MP3 player plugged into his ears all the time with Biggie, Jay-Z, Nas and Wu Tang on rotate.

B.R. returned the love and handed the empty plate to the lady waiting the tables.

The duo sat down and got right to business. "Flaco, check it. The last time I came through, the size 12 Nike Airs you gave me were perfect. Since then, I added a little height to my stature and my shoe size increased. I'll probably stop growing, for many different reasons, but for right now, I need a size 20. I know you wear a 16, that was established already. But since I've been growing, I forgot what size you were and accidentally copped you a size 14." B.R. pulled a pair of cocaine white 1's from a Sammy's Fashion shopping bag, showed them to Flaco then placed them back into the bag and continued, "my bad, but I do think that it's an even trade. 20 for 14 sounds like music to both of our ears. What do you think?" B.R. had his elbows on the table while his hands sat clasped in front of him.

Flaco let out a loud laugh and in a mimicking manner said, "Damn, son. I ain't know you knew Math like that. Let me find out you's a 5 percenter. Peace God, Peace God." Then he leaned in close to B.R. with a serious facial expression and studied those green eyes. A smile eventually made its way between Flaco's cheeks and remained there as he spoke. "All day, Son. All day, ya heard." Flaco embraced B.R. again and the two stood up at the same time.

"Same Bat time." B.R. sang.

"Same Bat channel." They both chanted at the same time.

With that, B.R. hopped in his whip and took the scenic route over to 450 East 169th Street. En route to the '9', B.R. let 50 Cent hypnotize him with some mix tape shit, *"I done been to the pearly gates, they sent me back/the good die young, I ain't never too old for that…"*

Chapter Eight

After B.R. returned from seeing Flaco, it was back to business as usual. 450 was clicking like the *Carter* from *New Jack City* and the fiends were rotating like inmates at a halfway house. B.R. and his team had eight apartments in 24 hour use with each spot holding down a specific job.

There were two apartments facing the front of the building, on opposite ends of the hallway, on two separate floors. The spot on the fifth floor was a look out haven which also held singles and five dollar bills. The spot on the 8th floor, which sat at the opposite end of the long hallway, looked like a gun store. Handguns, Tec's and sub machine guns occupied the living room since those were the weapons most frequently used. And all twenty of B.R.'s workers kept hammers on them at all times. The toasts in the living room were extra.

In one bedroom, A.K. 47's lined one wall, S.K.S.'s and 30-30's lined another, while the wall adjacent the bedroom door was laced with shotguns of every make and modification.

The second bedroom looked like an old bunker. Piles of Army fatigue suits in all sizes were scattered everywhere. In one corner sat a huge chest with the word *Grenades* spray painted on its side.

The third floor apartment faced the back of the building, looking over at 168th Street. Nickels of crack the size of multi-vitamin pills were sold from that location. On the sixth floor, also facing the back of the building, was an apartment that held $20's, $50's and $100 dollar bills. Two of the other four apartments were on the top floor and were occupied by senior citizens. All the coke was kept there. The last two apartments were chill out spots. The crew would meet up there to kick it, count money, re-up and watch videos.

Sitting in front of the building on the bench facing the traffic, Lil Hahmo, Lil K.I. and B.G. were scheming on some pussy and were discussing who was gonna get fucked next.

"Son, you hear me?" Hahmo was hollering at K.I., who was sitting to his left. "That bitch Tamika from 1-7-0 and Third got a head game like a fish. Shorty don't come up for air until you do."

"That's the broad you be calling a catfish? 'Cause she do look like a cat, with her skinny ass face." K.I. assumed. There were two Tamika's on 170th street and Third Avenue but K.I didn't know which one his homie was pluggin'.

"Yeah, that's the Mika I'm talkin' 'bout."

"I thought you was calling shorty a fish 'cause her pussy stank." B.G. interjected. B.G. was burnt out and usually thought outside the box, especially when it came to girls. When it was drama, his ratchet banged like a coal miner in a tunnel. But when it was time to get bitches, B.G. went the simple route. He paid like he weighed.

"Nigga, I don't fuck stink pussy, that's your nasty ass brother. He keep a bum ass, dirt bomb, 4 chicken wing eatin' hoodrat on speed dial."

"Fuck outta here." Hahmo defended himself.

"What about nasty ass Kim from up on College. That bitch got like nine kids."

"Six," Hahmo cut Lil K.I. off and corrected his count at the same time. "*And* she look like LisaRae. She just got some big ass hips."

"Big hips my ass, that bitch is huge. Like three of her kids were made in a festival in Auburn. The nigga Baby T told me he smashed, and that Lil' girl look just like Son. I think the other two is from that crackhead nigga Trey-Bag from Lambert projects."

"You wouldn't hit it?" Hahmo questioned K.I.

"Shorty do got a donkey. And that stand, yo. Kim got the mean double jointed jumpoff." B.G. daydreamed.

"I be having her fat ass ankles kissing her ears, too." Hahmo boasted.

"What's up for tonight, though?" B.G.'s dick got hard thinking about Kim's toes touching the back of her neck. He wanted some pussy, whether it was from Kim, Tamika or whoever.

Hahmo looked at B.G. as he peeled himself from off of the bench and faced his two siblings. He lifted his leg, placed his foot on the bench and looked K.I. in his eyes.

K.I. smiled, adjusted his semi hard on and said, "What," followed by a quick giggle.

"What's up with them old head bitches from Edenwald?" Hahmo remembered the Edenwald experience. It was one he couldn't forget.

B.G. said, "Hold up," hopped off the bench and started searching himself. A second later he pulled out his wallet that was rubber ban connected to a beat up phone book. He pulled out a sticky page and bellowed, "Ooh, Veronica,

Veronica, Ooh, Veronica gurl."

The trio erupted into a group laughter because Veronica was part of an old head team of cokehead broads that went super hard. One day Veronica licked all of their asses on a stage on 229th Street in front of the Housing police station in Edenwald on Edenwald Day for a dime of powder. B.G., Lil Hahmo and Lil K.I. were 16 years old at the time and that was two years ago. Veronica, Roxanne and Shante were in their early thirties. They lived on the same floor as each other in building 1141 on the northside of the housing development.

"Hold up," Hahmo said and pulled out his cell phone. He entered a number, heard a couple of beeps, and then pressed the chirp button on the side of the Nextel. *Bloop! Bloop!* The phone sounded.

"How you know those bitches got their phone on?" K.I questioned as they waited for a response.

"Watch." Hahmo stated.

"Hello," Roxanne spoke into her phone.

"Told y'all. Them bitches stay thirsty. Watch this," Hahmo assured like if he knew what was coming next. "Roxy," he said into the speaker.

"Hahmo, is that you?"

Hahmo started laughing, then he held his composure. "Yeah, this Hahmo."

"V, knock on Shante door, this Hahmo and 'em." Roxanne was so excited that she didn't realize she still had her chirp button applied. Even if she did know, shorty went hard. She didn't give a fuck if Bush was listening. Hahmo and them heard the geeking in her voice and mentally prepared themselves for a night of freaking off. "Y'all coming through or what?" she asked.

"We didn't call to say hi."

"What time y'all coming then?"

The trio giggled again at Roxanne's persistence until K.I. couldn't take it anymore and ran up the block laughing.

• • •

"That's one of them faggot ass niggas right there." A voice spoke from the interior of an old police car. The vehicle was parked on the bridge on 169th Street that overlooked the Metro North train track right next to Park Avenue.

"You wanna get duke?" the driver of the sedan fingered his 9mm and eyed Lil K.I.'s movements.

The front of the building had about 15 people standing around and sitting in front of it. The occupants of the Mercury, one being dude who escaped in the Cherokee when Hahmo and K.I. shot it up, knew they couldn't run up on anyone in front of the building and get away with it. 450 was like Fort Knox, and last week's incident proved it. The duo had a better chance watching from a distance like they were, and catching any one of their rivals out of the area and out of their comfort zone, than walking up in front of 450 on a suicide mission.

"Nah, Son, let's chill. When they move, we move."

"Just like that?"

"Just like that."

• • •

"Give us like an hour," Hahmo told Roxanne.

"Y'all gonna bring suttin?" Veronica jumped into the conversation.

"You tossing salads?" B.G. threw out there since everyone was being up front.

"Who that? B.G.?" Veronica asked.

"Yeah," B.G. confirmed.

"Youngin, I'm gon' toss yo' salad, suck the Cocoa butter off yo' big dick and let you fuck any hole yo' young ass can bust off in. Then me and my girls gonna switch. We got a cereal box full of Viagra's, Cialis and condoms, and a bucket full of K.Y. Jelly. If y'all lil niggas got the energy, we'll see y'all in an hour." *Bloop! Bloop!*

"It's on, son," Hahmo told B.G. "Yo, K.I." He called out to his other sibling.

"Yo."

"Go and get the Impala. We ready to roll, *now*."

"No doubt."

Two minutes later, K.I. pulled a black, limo tinted Impala SS, up to the curb of the building. A few words were exchanged between the triplets and a number of people in front of the building then B.R. appeared. He gave each of the brothers some dap and watched them as they pulled off. A moment later he too disappeared back into the building.

When the Impala got halfway down Park Avenue heading towards 170th Street, the hidden Mercury flicked it's ignition, reversed, then pulled into the flow of traffic a few cars behind K.I. and his brothers.

"Follow them niggas, Son."

"No doubt."

Chapter Nine

When K.I., Hahmo and B.G. pulled up in front of Veronica's building, the stoop was jam packed with niggas hustling, shooting dice and chilling. What always amazed the trio was how Housing supplied two big ass apartment buildings with a tiny fifteen car parking lot. Half of the time the parking spaces remained empty because disrespectful residents would use the tenant's vehicles as beds and benches. At any given moment, groups of dudes could be found sleeping on the hood or trunk of a parked car or stashing their illegal belongings in the wheel's well.

The Impala the threesome arrived in had a mean system in it. When the youngsters eased into a parking space and took their time placing their firearms on their person, the crowd of twenty or thirty individuals that loitered in front of and on the benches in between 1135 and 1141, turned the front of their living quarters into a small party.

B.G was the first to exit the car, from the rear, where the majority of the speakers were located. True indeed, Lil Hahmo, Lil K.I. and B.G. were from New York City and repped it unquestionably hard, but they still enjoyed all kids of music. Young Dro was telling everybody in earshot to

Shoulder Lean, on some ATL shit. Hahmo, K.I. and B.G. were feeling the newcomer's single and decided to let it play out. K.I. noticed that the crowd was enjoying the tunes just as much as he and his brothers were so off of response and reflex, he popped the trunk and got things cranking, *"My girl got a girlfriend, Chevy blue like whirlwind,"* Young Dro chimed in his southern twang.

"Ayo son, what the fuck is that!?" Hahmo pointed with an upward nod of his head in the direction of three little girls doing something he never saw displayed anywhere else.

B.G. smiled because on many occasions he'd trip off of Amiaya and her little crew of girls doing the same dance. "That's the Chicken Noodle Soup."

"The what?" Lil K.I. inquired. He heard what B.G. had said but he wasn't sure if what he heard was correct. *I know this nigga didn't just call that shit the Chicken Noodle Soup.*

"They call that the Chicken Noodle Soup. Watch this," B.G. waited fort his favorite part of the dance, then joined in with the girls from where he stood at in the parking lot, "Chicken Noodle Soup, Chicken Noodle Soup, Chicken Noodle Soup with a soda on the side. Now let it rain, and clear it out."

Hahmo and K.I. looked at each other. K.I. closed the trunk and front passenger door. Hahmo closed the driver's side door and B.G. closed the back door. Then Hahmo hit the alarm. Hahmo and K.I. looked at B.G. who was peering over at both of them smiling. Then at the same time, Hahmo and K.I. told B.G. "You're burnt the fuck out!"

With that, the trio proceeded towards the entrance of 1141, throwing up the 'B' sign, Eastsidin' Bloods and Bloodettes, and giving dap to everybody else they knew.

"Yo Ray, what's good, son?"

Lil Hahmo was hollering at one of the last men standing from the early 90s generation. Ray had had a long run in the streets that had been recently interrupted by a military style skid bid. For seven months he jogged, sang and did push-ups, pull-ups and dips upstate, with his 6 foot frame that no longer tipped the scale at close to 350lbs. He had been home for a good six months and still maintained his glow.

"What's poppin' baby boy, you stayin' out of trouble?" Hahmo was inquiring whether or not Ray was thinking about getting his feet wet again knowing that it was hard to cheat on the drug game once you tied the knot with it.

Ray smiled, "I'm good, ya heard. Good lookin' though, and if I need to get my head right, you know my brother is gonna take good care of me."

"I know that's right. Where's the Godfather at anyway? I ain't seen son since his wedding."

"He told me y'all turned it out."

"Nah, we were on our best behavior." Hahmo cheesed.

"I ain't talking about that." Ray guided the question.

"Oh yeah, well, you know. Your brother never said how many niggas we could bring. So, I figured."

"70 niggas, son. 70!"

"What can I say. Bloods rule." Hahmo laughed at his own comment. "But yo, tell Ruler I got them 036's ready to transform and roll out, ya heard. I just sent my G-Shine that's up there with Ruler a kite, asking what's up. I mean whatever. Shit, them alphabet boys ain't stopping nothin'. The kids gotta eat so the show must go on."

"I feel you. I'll tell him you hollered,"

"You do that!"

"Y'all going to see o'l girl and them," Ray looked up at

Veronica who was squashed in between Roxanne and Shante, looking out of Veronica's kitchen window.

Lil Hahmo placed his finger at his lips and said, "Shhh!"

Ray giggled and said, "One!"

"All the time." The trio said in unison and skipped into the building.

• • •

"What chu' tryna do, lay for them niggas?'

"Might as well." The Cherokee survivor spat.

• • •

"Hold up, wait." Veronica debated.

B.G. was standing over Veronica's face with nine inches in his hand that needed to get burped.

Lil Hahmo was laying up under her, stroking away with six of his nine inches up her ass trying to give her an enema.

Lil K.I. was on top, positioned like a crab, digging up in Veronica's front love tunnel like if his performance would garner him an Oscar.

B.G. ignored Veronica's pleas and shoved his Jimmy deep into her mouth until it touched her tonsil. He grabbed the back of her head with both hands and fucked the drool out of her face.

Roxanne and Shante were in the bathroom inhaling an 8-ball of Flaco's finest, twitching and talking 100 miles an hour about nothing.

"Girl, wha chu' doing later?"

"Shit, nothing." Shante replied after a sniff. " This shit good, aint it?"

"Mm hmm."

The three amigos helped the chicks get three nuts off.

The youngins skidded off twice and was good. A gram and a half and two C-notes was left behind to equate the bill and plans were made for a remix session. The trio exited the building two hours later with a blunt floating amongst the three of them as they reminisced about the freak off episode that just went down.

• • •

"Heads up." The Cherokee survivor said to his partner. "Pull up next to these marks like that Muslim nigga did Biggie."

• • •

"Ayo you hear me. All you have to do is put it next to Shante's pussy and home girl will cum, *instantly*." Lil K.I. joked.

About five feet from the Impala, B.G. stopped and said, "Blood, was it me, or did Roxanne's under arms smell like mine?"

K.I. and Hahmo were bent over in laughter and since B.G. had his back turned to the curb, nobody noticed the burgundy tinted out Grand Marquis pull up with the back window rolled down.

A shotgun peeked out the window about a yard away from B.G.'s back and blew him a kiss, *Bloom!*

K.I. and Hahmo ducked and caught only the tail of the getaway car as it hopped down the street.

B.G. was lying on the ground with his eyes wide open taking short, quick breaths.

Both K.I. and Hahmo ran over to their brother and hugged him hard. B.G. was dying, there was no doubt about it. Guts, a lung and some of B.G.'s liver was on the bottom of the wrought iron gate near the chess tables in front of the building.

They passed their pistols off to Ray and told him to hold them down until they came back for them.

"Yo, y'all had beef with some Jamaican niggas?" A Panamanian kid named Box that lived in the building asked Hahmo after he trotted over.

"Not that we know of, why?" Hahmo asked, upset and still holding on to B.G.

"I buy smoke from some dread niggas who push a Grand Marquis the same color as the one that just murked up outta here."

"Shit, that could've been anybody." Lil K.I. said, now standing to his feet.

"Yeah, but there's only one burgundy Grand Marquis in New York with California tags on it. At least that *I* know of." When the ambulance and the police showed up, Box winked at K.I. and added, "When y'all come back to pick up what y'all left behind, I'll be out here waitin'. Go do what y'all have to do, I'll holla. One!"

"One!" K.I. and Hahmo said at the same time and hopped in the ambulance with their brother.

Chapter Ten

A month had gone by since B.G.'s funeral and B.R. was sitting in front of his building thinking about the good times he had with his comrades. A pair of Macaroni and Cheese Gortex adorned his feet while a beige Sean John velour sweat suit kept his body warm from the cool breeze. Uptown in Edenwald, and downtown on the 'nine,' a mural of B.G. was painted on the side of one of the buildings in his memory by a kid from Westchester named D-110%. D-110% was Italian and from the burbs but was mean when it came to tagging up graffiti on the walls and on trains.

B.R. had two homies posted up directly across the street from him rocking back and forth on a chain link banister that had been installed to keep feisty children off the grass.

Two more workers were seated together in a hooptie that didn't start, on the corner of 169th Street and Park Avenue, facing 170th Street. Another two workers were laying in the cut by the deli on Washington Avenue.

B.R. was two-waying his people up in Edenwald to see if they had yet to secure an address on the perps who murdered B.G. A set of tiny hands suddenly appeared and covered B.R.'s eyes right after he sent the message.

"Amiaya, stop playing." B.R. said, maintaining his somber like demeanor.

Amiaya sucked her teeth and walked around the concrete ornament until she was standing in front of him. B.R. placed his two-way on vibrate, put it on his hip, and looked up at Amiaya. She had her arms crossed under her chest and for a moment, it looked as if Amiaya had a set of 17 year old titties. Amiaya's hair was braided in two long pigtails and she had on a pair of tight, Baby Phat jeans.

B.R. stared at Amiaya until she spoke up. She smiled, and for the first time in a long time, she didn't utter anything that sounded immature. "Why you sitting out here by yourself?" Before B.R. could answer her, she placed herself in the space next to him, pulled and snapped the bottom of her bra, because it had risen up too high, and continued, "You thinking about B.G.?"

B.R. felt her staring at him but continued eyeing the cars that drove past him. He licked his lips, looked over at Amiaya, paused, then looked back out into the street and calmly asked, "What is it to you?"

Amiaya shrugged her shoulders, sighed and responded, "B.G. was cool as shit."

B.R. looked back at her and Amiaya knew it was because she had just swore, so she told him, "I curse when I'm sad or upset, and my mother's aware of it. She doesn't like it but she knows that I ain't ten years old anymore." Amiaya looked at B.R. because when she mentioned her age, it was supposed to strike a cord somewhere. It didn't, from the look on his face, so she continued, "B.G. was my nigga too and I know that was your boy. I can imagine what you're going through." She kicked her feet in front of her and examined her shoes. She had on the same boots that B.R. had on. B.R. looked

ANTOINE "INCH" THOMAS

down at them and chuckled, then he looked at his boys across the street from him and with his eyes, asked then if they were okay. They responded with a tap on their chests that told him they were good.

After the pause, Amiaya placed her hand on B.G.'s and asked, "So y'all gon' get them niggas?"

She looked up at him nervously because she was beginning to feel warm inside. The feeling had nothing to do with B.G.'s death. Amiaya was feeling warm inside because she really liked B.R., on some boyfriend and girlfriend shit. B.R. was legally grown and in a month or so, Amiaya would become a teenager. She knew that B.R. cared about her like an older brother would if she had one, but she wanted him to *like her*, like her. She knew that he didn't have a girl and she knew that she was too young to date, but if she could be 18 for one day, she'd ask him if she could be his girl and have him promise her that he'd always be in her life.

B.R. placed his other hand on top of Amiaya's. Her smile broadened to its limit. When B.R. faced her, he spoke slowly, "Amiaya."

Amiaya said, "Yes," so fast that it connected with him calling *her* name and almost sounded like the two were singing. Amiaya was breathing hard and almost cried when B.R. made his next move.

B.R. gently removed Amiaya's hand from his, sat it in her own lap and explained, "Babygirl, you're twelve, and I'm gon' always see you as a twelve year old." He crushed all of her hopes of being with him. To add insult for emphasis, without further explanation, he got up, pulled out his phone and started walking off.

Amiaya hopped up, stormed into the building, arms still folded, attitude on blast then made a u-turn and headed his

84

way. As B.R.'s call was going through, Amiaya walked back up on him, placed her hands on her hips and yelled, "Nigga, you gon' be my man one day! So let all these bitches know," she looked at her Mickey mouse Jacob watch that B.R. had bought her for Christmas. Then she looked back up at him. "I'll be sixteen in three years and two months, then you're mine. So get ready nigga." She promised as she walked away. When she got to the entrance of the building, she stopped, turned around again and spoke with her watch hanging from her hand. "This Mickey Mouse shit is for the birds. A boss's wife should have on a Rollie. And I want mine flooded with pink diamonds."

"Who was that?" Dude on the other end of B.R.'s conversation asked him.

"My pride and joy. Now tell me what you got."

As he continued the conversation on his Nextel, Amiaya stood in the doorway with her finger applied to the 'Hold' button. She waited until B.R. turned and looked in her direction once more, then she let the elevator door close and take her to her destination.

"I got an address where them Cali Rasta niggas be at. You got a pen?"

"I don't need one." B.R. said sternly.

"Ahight, they be at 2311, East 183rd street on Southern Boulevard, inside the block. They be in a building with a gated entrance that look like a prison cell. The one who more than likely pulled the trigger, his name is Chocka. A skinny nigga wit' dreads, brown skinned, about my height with a bad attitude. His man is an American dude named Kendu. Real skinny, light skinned with freckles on his face. Dude is from Highbridge off of University Avenue, but he be with the Chocka nigga everyday on 183rd street. Be careful though.

The Kendu nigga has been about his business since the 80's. There's been a lot of rumors circulating about slim's body count."

"Will it be hard to spot this Kendu nigga."

"Not really."

"Why not?"

"'Cause the nigga got green eyes just like you."

There was a slight pause before B.R. said, "Where you at right now?"

"I just made a sale so right now I'm coming out the back staircase of 1135 and I'm about to walk over to 1141 and kick it to Ray and them."

"You driving?" B.R. asked him.

"Nah, not yet. I just came home so I'm trying to get back on my feet first."

"You see a green Lex in the parking lot?"

Box stopped in his tracks and zero'd in on a green GS 300. "Yeah, I see it. Who's is it? Yours?"

"Nah, that's you. Ray got the keys." Box looked over at Ray who had the keys dangling from his fingers while he played in some chick's pants that was sitting next to him. "It's a big 8 in the trunk for you too, under the spare tire. The title is the glove. Get ya head right, ya heard. Then come and see me when you're ready to spend."

"Good lookin' son, holla if you need me."

"No doubt. Just keep it one-hunit."

"Word, one hunit."

B.R. closed his phone, cupped his hands over his mouth and with all the excitement and strength in his body yelled, "BLOOOD UP!!"

Chapter Eleven

Amiaya was inside her bedroom, in her mirror, practicing some of the latest dance moves. Her mother and Flower were in the living room talking about the Heart Foundation and whether or not Flower would remain retired. Flower wasn't actually retired. In fact, she was at her Empire State Building, corner office everyday. She'd counsel and advise patients and subordinates through meetings, phone calls and E-mails, and would set up and organize events supporting the same cause, for the people who worked under her.

"Mmph!" Amiaya grunted. She seemed to be able to perfect every dance routine that she saw on T.V., in the streets or at school. She had a five disc CD changer as part of her Bose entertainment system that Flower had given her for her eleventh birthday. Rosalyn had laced her daughter's bedroom the way Amiaya's mature mind had wanted it to look.

For those who were allowed to enter her private domain, Amiaya had her personal space looking like a bedroom out of Architectural Digest. The floor was covered by a 1 1/2 inch thick slab of pink carpet that matched Amiaya's bed spread, comforter, curtains and lamp shade. Her full size bed was supported by a rusty brown, Rosewood head and foot, flower designed baseboard. A rusty brown Rosewood six drawer bureau, full of panty and bra sets, socks and head scarves, took up a portion of one wall while a look alike, semi-long twelve drawer; three level dresser lined the other.

Amiaya had a floor to ceiling mirror right next to her stereo, where she went over routines like rappers did their lyrics in a booth. With the encouragement of G-Unit, Beyonce, Jay-Z and Ciara through their music, Amiaya just knew that she was America's Next Top Mami.

At the moment, her favorite rapper was getting rich, dissing the shit out of his enemy on her two 12" house speakers. *You hire cops to hold you down, 'cause you fear for your life.* As the song progressed, Amiaya, in a pair of pink foot-less H&M tights, a white scoop-neck ENYCE long sleeve t-shirt with a hood attached to it and a pair of white bootie socks with a puffy pink ball hanging from the rear of them, popped, locked, leaned, dropped, jerked and shook like a high paid, feature video chick.

Amiaya loved G-Unit and the aggressiveness they portrayed. She was an aggressive young chick herself and felt comfortable listening to music that was compatible with her. *And yo' boss is a bitch if he could he would, sell his soul for cheap, trade his life to be Suge.* Amiaya was silly though, because although she admired 50 Cent for his musical creativity, drive and ambition, she often wondered, *how the hell you can be the hardest in New York, when it was you who took nine in the face and ass.* No homo.

Amiaya's telephone rang and when she looked at the caller ID, she recognized the number as someone who she didn't really like or want to speak to. It was funny how she would give her number out to different dudes just to free-rec, and dudes would sometimes think they had a shot at the title.

People couldn't front, Amiaya was a pretty young thang, with an amazing set of eyes. Unlike her mother, she had an ass that put old niggas in a jailbait state of mind.

For a moment, she stopped and admired herself in the mirror. She was thankful for her full chest, courtesy of Rosalyn's side of the family, but could never understand why B.R. wouldn't take her seriously. She was 12, but would be 13 in like 45 days, and knew about everything criminal that went on in or around 450 East 169th Street.

The phone rang again, snapping Amiaya out of her trance. She lowered the volume on her stereo, plopped down on her bed, picked up her phone, pulled her hoodie on to her head and stated, "I hope you not calling a bitch to waste my time."

Pharell, the dude on the other end of the phone, was a 14 year old cornball, fake Blood nigga that looked like the super producer himself. Amiaya met him on the Bx #41 bus about a week prior, told him that he was cute, that he looked like the Virginia muiltimillion dollar musician and gave him her number. Ever since then, o'l boy rocked the name like if it was typed on his birth certificate. *Bird.* Plus he was getting short paper selling nickels in Crotona Park, right across the street frion the Bronx state prison halfway house.

The way Amiaya answered the phone caught the homie off guard so he said, "Yo," he paused for a second as he looked at the phone, then at his boy sitting next to him. He placed the horn back to his face and continued, "Can I speak to Ameeyah?"

"It's Amiaya nigga, can't chu' read?'

"Hold up shorty. This ya boy, Pharell. I ain't one of ya lil,"

"Clown!" Amiaya chopped his sentence before he could finish.,

"Clown?"

"Yeah, nigga! You's a fuckin' bird, calling yourself some soft ass rapper."

"Hold up, ma. First of all, my name Murder. Bloody Murder. I go's hard and I gets that paper. I usually slap bitches that come at me sideways and they ain't my hoes,"

Click!

Amiaya hung up the phone on his ass.

Dude called her right back.

Ring!

"Hello," she said without looking at the caller ID. Her face was balled up because she couldn't believe how much of a derelick dude was.

"Listen here you fuckin' slut!"

"Slut?"

"Yeah, bitch! Slut! Smut!"

"Bitch? Do you know who I am?" She screamed. "Do you know who the fuck my people's are, nigga?"

"Yeah, them niggas gon' all be dead, along wit' yo' stink ass as soon as I see you. You bum bitch. I'm from Fulton Avenue, hoe!"

"And I'm from 450. The '9', nigga. Bring ya' pussy ass around here and watch you get dealt with."

Murder pressed the end button on his cell, looked over at his Puerto Rican homie and said, "Shoot me over to the Nine real quick."

"That's where that bitch live at?" Papo asked. Papo was average height, about a buk 50, maybe a buk sixty, with a wet jacket and soggy boots on, and looked like a beat up Sylvester Stallone. He was also type slow, due to all the Dust that he ingested, but for the moment, he was as sober as an alcoholic.

Murder was about the rap nigga, Pharell's height and weight, but was a lot grimier looking. He had a .25 automatic on him with four kids in the clip and one in the stomach. He had shot and killed a pitbull on Tremont and Park Avenue, right in front of Frank's Army and Navy, one time and thought that he was gangsta after that. Plus his man Papo kept lying to him and boosting his ego by calling him an O.G., when son was just a peon. If you're a Blood and you're an O.G., you done put in enough work to be considered G'd up and definitely a shot caller.

"Yeah." Murder confirmed Amiaya's location to his man. "Let's go."

With that, the duo hopped up in a beat up four door, two toned blue, Chevy Citation that they copped from a fiend for twelve nickels that they said were dimes.

In the crib, Amiaya re-wrapped her doobie and put on a pair of pink and white, canvas and suede Air Max. As she smothered her wrap with a Fendi head scarf, 50 gave her the boost she needed as she headed out the front door mimicking his lyrics, *Stay the fuck outta my zone, outta my throne, I'm New York City's own, Bad Guy.*

Chapter Twelve

"Son, what's good for tonight?" Kendu spoke to Chocka. Kendu and Chocka were posted up in the courtyard of their building hitting licks from the five pounds of smoke they broke down into $20's.

Chocka had his dreads secured by a large black, yellow and red, wool crown that most people called a *Jamaican Hat.* He had on a pair of Desert Storm beige and brown Army fatigue pants, a pair of construction Timbs and a black t-shirt.

Kendu was sitting on a crate with a pair of blue Georgio Armani jeans, a white t-shirt with an image of a book cover called *That Gangsta Sh!t,* silk screened into its fabric and a pair of low top, white on white, Air Force One's on his feet. Kendu had a brand new chrome .45 with a black rubber handle in his waistline, fiddling with a blunt as he and his man kicked it.

"Ain't shit poppin' off tonight. I'm supposed to go through Co-Op City, section 5, to see if this kid still want the 20 pounds he asked me about. He seemed legit, but I just wanted to make sure." Chocka announced.

Just then, two little kids used their key to enter into the

courtyard. They jogged past Chocka and Kendu laughing and joking about either the action figures that one kid had in his hands, or the PSP that the other kid wasn't trying to let go of.

Chocka and Du ignored the youngsters and continued with their conversation.

Chocka had a damp rag with him that he kept applying to his face with hopes of getting rid of the stye that had suddenly formed on his eye.

"B.R., you good, Blood? You ain't said nothing the whole ride over here." Hahmo checked with his homie from the back seat of a stolen black 1993 4-door Eddie Bauer edition Ford Explorer.

"I'm good. I'm just thinking about something." B.R. was behind the wheel with his eye on two little kids chasing each other up and down the block. One of the kids had a Superman action figure in one hand and in the other, Spiderman looked like he was about to fall apart. The other kid looked like he was gripping a newer model Gameboy or something.

Hahmo looked behind him at K.I. who was getting dressed. "You good, baby brah?"

"I'm good, Blood. Yo, you hear me?"

Hahmo was about to turn away but brought his attention back to K.I. who had his hand up.

With a connection only a set of twins could understand, Hahmo took K.I.'s hand into his, threw up the 'B' and said, "Eastside."

"All the time." K.I. concluded.

"Let's go!" B.R. said when the two little kids that were running up and down the block walked back by the truck heading for the entrance of the building.

"Yo, you hollered at Heather?" Kendu asked Chocka. Heather was a white broad from Pelham Manor that Chocka had met at a gas station near the Caldor's bridge on Boston Post Road. Heather looked like the average white chick, heavy on the foundation, lip liner and crystal blue eyes. She had blonde hair, drove a 1999 Honda Civic and had ass implants that looked like the real deal. Heather had a friend that Kendu had fucked once and was wondering what was up with her.

Hailey, the friend, sucked on Kendu's dick while they watched the movie *Heat*, from the time Tom Sizemore rammed the armored truck in the beginning, until Robert DiNiro and Al Pacino had that shootout near the airport runway. Hailey had come up for air once during her suck-a-thon.

"Hold up," she told Kendu as she palmed his nuts. His hand was gripping her blonde tresses as she watched her favorite part of the movie. Hailey had gone to an integrated school in New Rochelle for two years and thought that she knew what *gangsta* was. "Ashley Judd keeps it gangster right here when she gives Val Kilmer the signal that the cops have her. That's my girl." She smiled happily as she explained her reason for liking that part of the movie.

"Yeah whatever." Kendu said and guided her mouth back to where it belonged.

Chocka answered Kendu's question regarding Heather just as the two juveniles who had been running in and out re-entered the premises, followed by three Muslim ladies carrying groceries. Chocka figured the women to be Muslim because they had their faces covered with Hijabs, wore plain full length pull over robes and had prayer rugs slung over their shoulders. "I spoke to her last week." Chocka answered as his eyes followed the women.

B.R., Lil K.I. and Lil Hahmo waited until they stood parallel with the dude with the dreads tucked in his hat and the other skinny nigga with the brown hair and matching freckles on his face and neck. In a single movement, the grocery bags hit the floor and B.R., K.I., and Hahmo stood stationery with the fully automatic MP-7's in their hands looking like three kamikaze women fighting for their homes in Iraq.

"Oh shit!" Kendu yelled and started to run. He reached for his .45 as the bullets began their conversation.

Bttaatt! Bttaatt! Bttaatt!

B.R. and the crew swept the entire area with slugs that Kendu and Chocka had occupied. The bullets from K.I. and Hahmo's guns taught Chocka how to dance and glued him to the bars on the building's exterior.

Kendu thought that he had gotten away. He made it safely behind a concrete pillar and stood there with his pistol by his face, ready to squeeze. Time was of the essence so Kendu reached his hand around the pillar and let off four shots in the trio's direction without looking. He needed to make a run for the entrance of the building but was too shook to move.

B.R. caught Kendu's reflection in the building's window and knew exactly where he stood and what he was doing. B.R. ran up and stood on the opposite side of the same pillar and snuck a quick glance at the window again. He noticed that Kendu had a cell phone in his hand trying to make a phone call. The cannon Kendu had was under his armpit, making it easier for him to dial 9-1-1.

That was B.R.'s window of opportunity. He swung around the pillar and put the gun to Kendu's head. Du was scared to death. He didn't know what to do so he just closed his phone but kept his .45 secured by his side. He was shaking, he looked like he was about to cry *and* drop the gun.

"One!" B.R. said and pulled the trigger.

Bttaatt!

"Come on!" K.I. bellowed out to B.R. who was standing over Kendu's lifeless body.

B.R. looked around for the two kids that let them into the grounds, hoping that they were somewhere safe. He turned around, ran and grabbed the grocery bag. He slipped the mini machine gun back inside of it and casually walked back over to the Explorer.

Ten minutes later, the trio was pulling into the parking lot behind their building safe and sound.

Chapter Thirteen

Amiaya exited her building and was on her way to the store. Jay-Z was playing in the I-Pod she had strapped around her neck and the biography he was giving of himself was everyday life in the 'hood. To many of his suburban fans, the Shawn Carter claim to fame was a mere rhyme and reason. However, to those in the ghetto, the self proclaimed greatest rapper alive's rise to the top, was no walk through the projects. *Honey's used to say I was ugly and wouldn't touch me, then I rolled up in that dubbed out buggy,* was more of a summary of his struggle.

Amiaya admired the Jigga man for having the courage to share with everyone a story like *Song Cry.* Dudes who would eventually make it out of the 'hood via a draft pick or a connect and a town down south somewhere would almost never inspire others with their past experiences. Inside she praised Hov, *props were due,* and wished that more cats, on every level, would be more open minded to at least *imagine* success on the homey's level.

After the song finished and she was returning back to the front of her building, Amiaya was looking to improve the atmosphere to a more upbeat mood. Parties were usually about fun and having a good time, so Jay and his partner in rhyme, The Broad Street Bully, did their best to brighten up the moment, *Hat cocked can't see his eyes, who could it be?/wit' that new blue Yankee on, who but me,* they sang.

Just then a car pulled up and the occupants exited the vehicle. They slammed their doors with force and Amiaya heard when the second door connected with the frame of the old car. Just as she went to sit on a parked Buick in front of her building, she turned her head to be nosy and see who would treat their whip like it was a piece of shit.

"Fuck you got to say now, bitch?" Pharell/Murder approached Amiaya on some bullshit. His eyes were wide because Amiaya calling him a clown had son in his feelings. Dude was hustling, had guns too, other broads, and he was Damu. Those ingredients alone somehow told him that he deserved respect.

Amiaya pulled her headphones out of her ears and went to roll them around her I-Pod when Murder swung and slapped the shit out of her. *Bong!*

"Mutha-nigga, is, you- - fuckin'- - punk, bitch!" Amiaya managed to release partial sentences as she swung and kicked wildly at her assailant.

Murder was bobbing and weaving, swinging haymakers and uppercuts and everything was connecting. *Bing! Bong! Bam! Slap!*

B.R. said, "One." To Lil Hahmo and Lil K.I. after entering 450 from its rear. Hahmo and K.I. jetted up the stairs to re-stash their heat while B.R. walked into the lobby to check and make sure that everything was everything out front. A small crowd had formed as Amiaya did her best to represent the '9'.

She was kicking, scratching and trying to grab Murder but he was too quick and experienced for her.

One of B.R.'s workers recognized that it was Amiaya who was fighting and started across the street at the same time that B.R. popped out of the building. B.R. noticed some Puerto Rican cat standing near the curb cheering on some cat that was giving the business to a broad like if she were a dude. B.R. realized the broad was Amiaya and before jumping out there, he did a quick assessment of the whole jumpoff. *One player + one cheerleader = two dumb muthafuckas.* There was a two man team violating Amiaya on unfamiliar territory. So the odds were against the enemy. B.R. didn't recognize Laurel and Hardy, nobody from the '9' did. So they were out of bounds. *It ain't where you're from it's where ya at.* B.R. gave one of his workers the signal to get at Papo while he snuck up on Murder.

The worker crept up on the side of Papo and dead armed him. *Bong!* Papo stiffened up and slowly slid down the side of the whip that he was standing next to. Two more workers joined their partner and stomped the *mirra-mirra* shit out of Papo.

B.R. had a loose, long stem Gem star razor in the miniature pocket that sat inside of his right front pants pocket. He retrieved the weapon and walked behind Murder as Murder continued the assault on Amiaya. Amiaya didn't notice the help arrive because her long hair was all over the front of her face. All she knew was that she had to prevent dude from continuously making contact because the slaps were beginning to hurt.

At just the right moment, B.R. grabbed Murder in a headlock and squeezed him to calm him down. Murder complied because he wanted to turn around and see who the fuck wasn't minding their own business. For the few seconds that he dropped his guard, Amiaya snuck a punch and a kick in, right before one of the block huggers grabbed her and told her to be easy. B.R. released Murder while opening up his face from the top of the right side of his lip, to somewhere near the back of his hairline with the razor. *Sliiice!*

Papo had had the wind knocked out of him about 20 times during his stomp session so he was of no help to Murder. The Pharell look alike felt the incision and immediately grabbed his jaw.

A Housing Police beat walker was jogging toward the scene after nosy neighbors had alerted him that a fight was taking place on 169th Street. The officer was eating lunch at a pizza shop on 168th and Third Avenue when he was aggressively interrupted by a pedestrian.

"Yo, Cop! They fighting over on 169th Street." The woman yelled from the front door of the eatery.

"A fight? On 169th and what?" He asked as he laid his slice of pizza back on the counter, picked up his radio and walked briskly out of the small restaurant.

"Right there!" The lady said as she pointed through an open area behind the pizza shop.

The cop took off with his radio in his hand, describing what he saw, his current location, his estimated time of arrival on the scene and how much back up he'd need.

By the time the officer got close enough to determine that a simple fight wasn't all that was taking place, blood was dripping from a wounded kid's face and the instrument used was still in the attacker's hand.

"FREEZE!" The officer yelled. "Put it down! *Now!*"

"Fuck that!" *Pop, Pop, Pop!* Murder had his .25 pointed at B.R. and let off three shots. It was Murder who the cop was yelling at. B.R. fell to the ground holding his mouth and chest. The kid, more out of lack of control and shock, then aimed the gun at the cop.

Blocka!

The officer took Murder down with one shot to the head. B.R. was on the ground squirming with an injury to the face and torso. Amiaya was all over him. By now, Lil Hahmo and Lil K.I. had also appeared on the scene. The officer who shot Murder was trying to keep B.R. still and Amiaya up off of him before any interior damage could get any worse than it probably already was.

Other squad cars were arriving with anxious wannabe Rodney King cops ready to put a beaten on any uncooperative residents. The three dudes who had stomped out Papo had secretly drug him into the building and onto the elevator.

Flower and Rosalyn both exited the building in their housecoats. Flower was told that B.R. may have been the one who had gotten shot but she wasn't sure until the paramedics turned him over to be strapped down onto a stretcher. She recognized her baby boy immediately and collapsed right where she stood. Rosalyn, her best friend, was by her side to catch her.

"What happened?" She cried in Rosalyn's arms as she lay sprawled wildly on the ground.

"Shhh. He gon' be okay. AMIAYA! Bring yo' ass over here, girl!" Rosalyn too was bawling. She hated to see Flower in the state that she was in. It brought back too many memories. Plus there was about three dozen people outside sucking up misinformation to later start false rumors.

Amiaya ran over to her mom and Flower, and collapsed right next to Flower. "MAA!" She bellowed over her tears. "Is he dead?"

"Shhh!" Rosalyn tried to hush Amiaya too.

Just as B.R. was being lifted and rolled into the back of the ambulance and Amiaya and Flower were finally making it to their feet, Papo's body came crashing down onto the roof of one of the Housing Police cars that was parked on the side walk blocking the entrance to the building.

"Oh shit!" One bystander yelled. "They throwing niggas off the roof." He said as he looked up and caught a quick glimpse of someone pulling their head back.

The crowd dispersed like shots being fired outside of a club after it let out. Cops were ducking and drawing their pistols, some even ran into the building with hopes of catching the perps running down the steps or still on the roof. Flower, Rosalyn and Amiaya got up and walked across the street in case any more bodies were used to clear the area.

Flower looked at Amiaya and Rosalyn and embraced them once again with tears streaming down her face. They held her back and consoled her as much as they could. "My baby," she cried. "Rosevelt, not my baby."

Chapter Fourteen

18 Months Later

Flower walked up behind B.R., looked over his shoulder and looked at his face through the mirror. B.R. was at his home in Mt. Vernon with Flower, getting ready for his going away party. Flower had moved out of her 169th Street apartment and moved in with B.R. upon his request. Of course B.R. kept the apartment in 450.

"You look so handsome." She cooed. She fixed the collar on B.R.'s Dolce and Gabanna black leather Pea Coat and brushed down the smooth hair on the back of his head. Then she walked in front of him, admiring how long of a way he'd come. She was so happy at the man that he now was.

B.R. had on a pair of black, wide leg velour Armani slacks, a white short sleeve Armani linen button up with a pair of black Gucci loafers that kept his toes comfortable. Flower had water building up in her eyes because B.R. was about to turn himself in the following morning.

On the day that B.R. got shot, he also got charged with assault with a deadly weapon for cutting Michael Wilson, a.k.a. Bloody Murder, before his untimely death by a police officer.

Two of the three shots that Murder got off connected with its target. The first shot caught B. R. in the chin. The bullet entered, bounced off his lower jaw bone and exited out in almost the same spot that it had slipped into. The second shot missed him because B.R.'s head jerked back from the impact of the first slug to his face. The second shot was trying to have a meeting with his forehead. The third shot was an upper chest wound. The tiny portion of slug that *did* remain inside of his body, frequently changed locations, depending upon how B.R. moved around that day. Every time that it was foggy, misty or raining, the bullet enlarged inside of him brought uncomfortable pain to his entire body.

The party he was having for the evening, was an in house joint, family only. Flower rented out the Eastwood Manor, uptown on Boston Road. The spot was laid back and the atmosphere was real cool.

B.R. kissed Flower on the cheek and said, "I love you, mom. Don't worry, your boy is gonna be alright."

"I know." She cried and wiped her eyes with the sleeve of her nightgown. "I know. Now go have yourself a good time and make sure that Amiaya doesn't touch any alcohol." She forced a fake smile after her comment.

"I got you." B.R. trotted down the steps and hopped up in his whip. He stuffed his hammer in the stash spot up under the steering wheel and pulled his car into the street. While B.R. was on pre-trial fighting his case with the same lawyers that Irv Gotti and Lorenzo beat the feds with, he upgraded his Chrysler 300 to a Bordeaux Red CLS 500 Mercedes Benz.

When B.R. first heard the dealer mention the color, he

thought the guy was going to show him something that would look good on a low rider. So he asked the guy, "Excuse me, Mr. Murphy. Can you give me an idea of what Bordeaux Red looks like?"

"Maroon." Mr. Murphy had told him, "It's a $150,000 classy metallic maroon."

B.R. was trying to get his grown man on so he kept his 4-door coupe stock, and didn't tint his windows. The upholstery was cocaine white and from a distance, when the 500 was parked under a light, it looked like somebody had taken a bite out of a humungous apple.

B.R. had fought his case with a self defense strategy and ended up blowing trial to a simple assault. His attorney advised him to use his past as his defense which would've guaranteed him an acquittal by any jury. B.R. refused because that was no one else's business. He told his lawyer that after Flower had adopted him, his past no longer existed. So they stuck with the self defense theory and subsequently lost.

This was B.R.'s first time being arrested and the cop who shot Murder testified that B.R. was trying to defend himself. However, the facts remained that Murder was only 14 years old at the time of death and was assaulted *before* he pulled out the gun. The judge sentenced B.R. to 1½ to 4½, state time.

It was 11 p.m. and in less than twelve hours, B.R. would have to report to the Bronx Criminal Courthouse on 161st Street and Sheridan Avenue. He had to surrender himself to the authorities in Part 30. For a moment, B.R. thought back on the supportive words that his friends had given him after he had received his date to surrender.

"18 months ain't shit." Lil K.I. had voiced his opinion.

"You can do a year and a half standing on your head and beating your dick at the same time." Lil Hahmo did his best to make his homey's sentence seem like nothing.

"Baby, I'll be with you every step of the way." Flower had reassured him when he brought her the disturbing news.

At some point Rosalyn and Flower must have been discussing B.R.'s sentence and the date that he had to report in, when Amiaya apparently overheard the details.

"What!" she had mumbled to herself and went to look for her big brother / fantasy boyfriend / and future husband.

"Rosevelt," she had caught him in his mother's room packing the last of Flower's things to be moved up to Mt. Vernon.

"Yo," he said, looking at a photo of a young Flower at the club with an outfit on that should've only been made for some wife, fulfilling her husband's fantasy.

She plopped down on the bed next to him and said coyly, "I ain't know you blew trial." Amiaya was 14½ and had matured faster than anyone close to her would have imagined.

"Yeah," he confirmed, looking at another crazy photo of Flower. This time Rosalyn was in it and the two young ladies were holding up glasses of Champagne in one hand and stacks of money in the other. They both had on some Donna Karan outfits that looked outdated and real corny.

"Let me see my mother," Amiaya pulled B.R.'s hand so that the photo was in her face. "Oh, I saw those already."

"So why you asked to see it if you already saw them?"

"'Cause, I ain't know which one it was."

B.R. kept going through the stacks of photos when he suddenly felt Amiaya's hand rest on his thigh. Amiaya could've sworn that she felt him shudder so she figured that she had broken through his protective shield. She decided to lay it on thick. "Rosevelt, you know I'm gonna miss you, right?"

B.R. was gonna miss the hell out of her too but she would never hear it from him. "Word" is all he said.

"Yeah, nigga." Her hand had taken on a mind of it's own because before she knew what was happening, she was caressing his thigh. B.R. fought to focus but it was getting harder and harder by the minute. "I'ma write to you all the time and I'm gonna send you cards and pictures of me and my friends. I've been saving all that money that you've given me over the years and I'm gonna send you some of that too."

B.R. laughed and said, "I don't need no money, boo, I'm good. My people's got my tab. Just stay in school and out of trouble. You hear me?" His voice sounded like it was cracking.

When B.R. turned to face Amiaya she saw that he had tears streaming down his face. "Why you crying, Rosevelt?" She sounded so innocent. Amiaya had turned his face to hers and for some reason, he didn't try to hide his emotions this time. She bit her lip to prevent some of her own tears. Then she glued her eyes to his and emptied her heart out. "Rosevelt, When you come home I promise to have graduated at the top of my class. I promise that I will always respect my mother and that I will always check up on Flower for you. Whatever you need while you are in there, don't hesitate to ask me. Ain't no task too much for me to bear, like these sucka ass niggas keep crying about. *It's hard out here; I be too busy; I forgot; I'm broke,* fuck outta here wit' that corny ass shit." Amiaya too was crying. She was sniffling and soaking up her sleeve trying to ease the broken dam. "I'ma make sure these funky ass niggas stay in line around here and I promise that your car will stay clean and in impeccable shape." She had to laugh at the big word that she just used since she didn't normally talk that way, but she caught herself and picked up right where she left off at, "You need packages up there? The post office is right down the block. You need Timbs and an Army jacket? No need to stress Flower, I got you. I'm going to Frank's this weekend. And when you come home, if you still don't want me, I'm still gon' love you, 'cause you my nigga. You my boy, for real, Rosevelt."

"Amiaya, let me ask you something."

"You can." She nodded her head submissively.

"Did any of your teachers ever ask you what you wanted to be when you grew up?" B.R. dried his face with the back of his hand.

"Yeah. My first grade teacher, Mrs. Harding. She asked me what I wanted to be when I grew up and I'll never forget it because she sounded so sincere and concerned. Like if it really mattered to her what I wanted to be."

"What did you tell her?"

"I told her that I wanted to be Storm from the X-Men because she was too fly." They both laughed.

"And she went for that?"

"Nah, she said that Storm was fake and that I needed to pick a career choice, like what I wanted to work as when I got older."

"What did you end up telling her?"

"I said that I wanted to be like Flower because everyone always said she was special. What about you? Did your teachers ever ask you what you wanted to be?"

"Actually, it was my foster father who had once asked me that."

Amiaya noticed when B.R. blinked, that more tears had fallen, which meant that he had resumed crying. She didn't want to press the issue, but she was curious as to what he wanted to be when he grew up. "What did you tell him, Rosevelt?"

He didn't answer, he just shook his head and moistened his lips with his tongue.

"What did you want to be when you grew up, Rosevelt?" Amiaya grabbed his face and dried his tears. "Tell me."

"Dead." He answered her. "I wanted to be dead when I grew up."

Amiaya was about to say something when B.R. stopped her and said, "Just promise me one thing, ma." He had his finger on her lips. Then he pulled back and dug into his pocket.

"What, tell me." She damn near begged as she looked up at him.

"Promise me that you'll say yes on your 18th birthday."

What B.R. had said hadn't actually registered in Amiaya's brain because a statement like that could never exit his lips. When he tapped her and shoved a 3 carat, heart shaped, pink VVS solitaire diamond in her face, the reality of the moment went straight to her head.

With a smile so wide that it almost ripped her lips, Amiaya cheered, "What, nigga! You serious?"

The smile on B.R.'s face told her that he was *dead* serious.

Amiaya smacked him playfully on the arm once as she snarled, "Rosevelt, don't be playing with me."

His silence confirmed her dreams so she got up, hugged him and said real loud, "OH SHIT! I'm trippin'. Rosevelt, you got me buggin' out right now. This is crazy. For real? Don't be playing, nigga." She stood with her arms crossed, tears everywhere.

B.R. shook his head, further confirming the situation.

After a moment of thinking, she dove on him, forcing him on his back. Smiling brightly she said, "Yo, I got you, boo. Damn, Rosevelt. This is crazy. My dream nigga is finally giving in. Wait till I tell Mommy and Flower."

"Wait! Don't say anything to them. Keep this our little secret. We'll surprise them when it all pops off."

"So can I call you my man now, 'cause you *are* officially my man?" She couldn't stop cheesing.

"I guess."

"Fuck you mean, you guess?" She smacked him again. "You mine. Yes!" She licked her lips.

"Check it, take this ring and put it up until the time is right."

"You want *me* - - to put *this* - - whatever thousand dollar *ring* - - with the big ass rock in it - - *away* - - until you come home? Yeah *ah* - ight. This shit is going on my finger, right now." She slipped it on and modeled it. It fit perfectly. "*And it fit?*" She was animated again.

"Yo, I gotta go, ma. But I'ma holla at you when I come back from dropping off these boxes for moms." He tried to get up.

Amiaya pinned him back down and asked, "Can I have a kiss?"

"Turn your face."

"Turn my face?"

"Turn your damn face, Amiaya."

Amiaya turned her face and when B.R. went to kiss her on the cheek, she tried to put her lips on his but wasn't quick enough. B.R.'s kiss connected where it was supposed to land, then they got up. He packed the last box and left Amiaya to her own thoughts. Amiaya sat there for another hour, tripping about how her life had suddenly changed for the better.

That was two months ago. Now B.R. was trying to enjoy his last night on the town, a free man.

Chapter Fifteen

The Eastwood Manor

The evening was cool, the sky was clear and the club was stacked with around two hundred partygoers. Everybody in the place was dressed to impress. It was a formal get together so no sneakers or boots were allowed.

B.R. sat alone at a table fit for six people. The five other guests were up and about, jamming to the music and having a good time. When Ludacris finished ripping his hit single *Money Maker*, Beyonce took over and kept saying something about, *to the left—to the left.* Lil Hahmo and Lil K.I. took a seat by their homie while the fine women that they came with kicked it with Amiaya.

"What's good, Blood?" Hahmo stated as he made himself comfortable at the table.

"Chillin' kid." B.R. responded to Hahmo but was giving K.I. some dap as he sat down next to his brother and homeboy.

"What's good with y'all? Y'all two enjoying yourselves?" B.R. checked his peoples. Although it was a party celebrating the momentary departure of himself, he only agreed to it and attended the gathering so that his people could have a great time.

"We good, ya heard." Hahmo said and gave a toast to Cindy, the chocolate dimepiece that he had brought along to enjoy the evening with.

Cindy was on the dance floor with a Cosmopolitan in her hand dancing with Tia, Lil K.I.'s date, who also had a drink in her hand. K.I. followed his brother's lead and gave Tia an imaginary toast as well. The two young ladies were glowing, showing off their assets knowing that after the party was over, weaves and wraps were getting pulled and sweated out.

Cindy was dark skinned like Serena Williams and pretty like Puff's girlfriend Kim Porter. She was thick, had a mean ass, muscular legs and a walk that looked like she was dancing. She wore hazel contacts which made her eyes look daring and the Foxy Brown weave she sported made her long hair look like she was born with it. Cindy had on a pair of blue Seven jeans with a loose fitting sleeveless Gucci blouse that exposed some cleavage. The Gucci heels she rocked matched her purse but in a minute, all that fly shit would be slung over a chair in a hotel room while Cindy got the screws fucked out of her ass.

Tia was light skinned. Her dad was black, very handsome and her mom was Korean which is why she looked like a black woman with a pretty Chinese face. Tia had a chest like Meagan Goode and legs so long that dudes thought that she was all pussy. Her butt wasn't too big, firm and opened up whenever it needed to.

Tia had on a black D&G dress that hugged her body and made her look like a model. Her hair was done up and her makeup was flawless. She also had on a pair of D&G stilettos that made her height taller than Lil K.I.'s.

Tia and K.I. were seeing each other for about six months

and were really digging one another. After the second week, when K.I. had a taste of her milkshake, he realized that she wasn't all pussy. He had her crying and screaming and begging him to keep going. Tia was only 24 years old and when K.I. found out that he was only the third guy that she had been with, he asked her to be his girl. She gladly obliged and he had her on lock ever since.

The music switched over to a slow jam that Mary J. Blige had on her latest CD and that's when all three ladies decided to take a break and have a seat next to their respective dates.

Cindy walked over, kissed Hahmo on the lips and grabbed a chunk of crotch. She whispered something in his ear and afterwards they kissed again and both took a seat.

Tia walked up and had Lil K.I. drooling. She looked stunning in her outfit and she knew it. She gave K.I. a kiss when he stood up to meet her. She sucked on his tongue like it was candy. The two unlocked lips and sat down next to each other like they had been in love forever.

Amiaya was standing behind Tia and K.I. so when they sat down, her pretty face was in full view.

"Fix your face. They grown folk, ain't no need to be squinching up your grill like that." B.R. told her.

Amiaya said *whatever* to herself and made her way over to where B.R. was sitting. She stood over him, watching him, wondering when he was going to get up and give her a passionate kiss as well.

When B.R. noticed that everyone at the table was looking at him, he stood up, about a foot and a half taller than Amiaya, grabbed her face and kissed her on the forehead. Amiaya sucked her teeth, sat down next to him and reached for her drink. B.R. took it from her, slid it over to K.I. and slid her *his* glass of soda.

"My mom said not to let you drink anything that you're not old enough for." He looked at her. Amiaya had one of those, *No the hell he didn't* looks on her face.

"That's yo' momma, not mine. I'm trying to get my buzz on, so you better stop playing and pass me my drink back."

"Enjoy the Pepsi, Amiaya. Flower's only concerned about you, that's all."

"Please." She waved her hand.

For the rest of the evening everyone partied and enjoyed themselves. B.R. didn't get up and dance at all, instead, he remained on the sideline, eyeing Amiaya while she eyed him back. The red leather Fendi pants that were too tight for her prevented her from doing the dance moves she normally did at home. The red Chinchilla shawl she rocked also did little to hide her chest, while the high heeled Minolo's she sported minimized her movements to a simple two step.

When the evening came to an end at around 4 a.m., B.R. found himself sitting in a leather lazy boy in his room, watching Amiaya as she slept peacefully in his bed. He wondered if it would be a good idea to get with Amiaya when he came home. B.R. wasn't all there and could snap at any reaction, according to Mrs. Berkowitz, and he didn't want any of that behavior displayed toward Amiaya.

Before he jumped in the shower, he reasoned with himself: *I care about Amiaya too much to allow anything to happen to her. Before I'd ever hurt her, I'd leave.* With that, he walked into the bathroom and turned on the water. Amiaya lay in bed listening to the water hit the floor of the tub. She wiped her face because the tears had started again. She wasn't asleep when B.R. looked over at her, she was praying. She was asking God over and over to watch over her man and bring him back home in one piece.

Chapter Sixteen

Three Years Later

It was 9 a.m. and B.R. was on a bus headed south for New York City. He had been released earlier that morning from Southport Correctional Facility in Pine City, New York. In Southport every inmate that was housed there was in special housing, otherwise know as the hole. B.R. was commuting by way of bus as opposed to being picked up by some of his family members because he needed the idle time alone to think.

B.R.'s original sentence allowed him the opportunity to be eligible for release after serving only eighteen months, but ten days before he went to his first parole hearing, he jacked it off.

Flower, Amiaya and sometimes Rosalyn, would visit B.R. every other week at Greene Correctional Facility in Coxsackie, New York. On one particular visit, a week and a half before B.R. was scheduled for his parole meeting, Flower and Amiaya had come up to see him. Both women were dressed casual in slacks, short heels and loose fitting blouses because Greene had a strict dress code. Apparently one of the inmates that was on the visit recognized Flower from a job where she had been formerly employed.

Frank Smith #98B6760, a.k.a. Freaky Frank, a.k.a. Freaky Fo Sheezy, had paid Flower for a private session years ago when she danced at a strip club called The V.I.P. His man was visiting him and Freaky felt like he needed to impress his boy to remind him how it used to be when Freaky Frank was home.

Everybody on the compound, except for maybe a few dudes, including Freaky, who had recently been transferred to Greene, was aware of B.R.'s reputation. B.R. was on O.G. status in the jail and had been in two separate incidents which put him there. Those incidents also could have landed him and extra 10 to 15 years. In the first situation, one of his Bloods had left a red sweatshirt on a workout bench in the yard so that people would know that somebody was either using the bench, or about to use it. Some knuckle-head, young cat that had some big arms and a decent sized chest, decided to take it upon himself and move the shirt. When B.R. walked over, he noticed that the sweatshirt was on the floor like if it had been discarded there on some disrespectful shit. B.R. had a lot of sense and patience and knew that sometimes things weren't always what they seemed to be. So he approached the young fellow humbly and asked him, "Son, was that red sweatshirt right there," he pointed, "laying on the bench before you started your workout?"

Dude re-racked the weight, sat up, looked at B.R., then at the two dudes that were with him and lied with a straight face. "Nah, son. This bench was empty."

B.R. nodded his head and walked off. As soon as dude laid back down and picked the weight back up, B.R. smashed him in the head with a 45 pound dumbell. Understandably, the dude almost died and B.R. got away with it, but everybody on the compound knew what went down and who was responsible for putting in that work.

In the second incident, B.R.'s Army coat had been stolen from off of his bed one evening while he was in the shower. Usually when a sneak thief was on the prowl, the dude more than likely lived in the unit. It didn't take long for B.R. to find the culprit. He walked around the dorm checking the shoulder flap of every jacket until he found the one with his initials on it. He retrieved his jacket and waited until about 3 o'clock that morning. While the C.O. was counting sheep, B.R. boiled a bottle of Crisco oil and poured it on dude's bare chest and face. Again, word spread that B.R. would cook a nigga in a minute if you violated.

Back to the situation where Freaky played himself. Flower, Amiaya and B.R. were enjoying a tray of hot wings when Freaky suddenly approached their table.

"Excuse me, ma'am." He beamed at Flower. Freaky was taller than B.R. and much older than him as well, so respect was nonexistent. Plus he had about six years in on a 8 1/3 to 25 year sentence for possession of 200,000 bags of dope. He glanced over at Amiaya, licked his large lips, then he looked at B.R. and frowned his face up.

Flower figured that something was wrong and tried to defuse whatever was about to happen. She placed a comforting hand on B.R.'s arm, looked up at Freaky and asked, "Can we help you with anything, sir?" Flower's dancing days happened ages ago so it was hard to remember anybody from that time in her life.

Freaky had a toothpick in his mouth. When he brought his gaze back to Flower he twirled the stick around with his tongue then folded his arms across his chest. "Hey Angel, remember me?" He teased and grabbed the crotch area of his pants.

"Ma, you know this nigga?" B.R. asked Flower.

When B.R. looked into Flower's eyes he saw that the floodgates were about to open. So with all of his might, he swung and punched Freaky in the mouth. Freaky landed about 6 tables from where the punch connected. After a crucial beatdown by the C.O.'s for inciting a riot, B.R. was eventually shipped out to Southport box where he remained until he was released.

The bus stopped at Port Authority on 34th Street where B.R. then boarded a yellow taxi cab. He took the cab to 169th Street and Webster Avenue and walked up the hill to his building. It was around September, so it was still somewhat hot out. Girls were walking around with next to nothing on and dudes were driving by with their systems knocking. B.R. was taking it all in and could imagine what he had to look forward to, once he stepped in front of 450.

His plans were to holla at whoever was outside, then make his way up to Mt. Vernon. The last he heard before he went to the hole was that K.I. and Hahmo were copping their own work and holding a nice piece of change for him. Before he turned himself in, he explained to his connect what was jumping off and told Flaco that he'd holla when he touched down. Since then though, his thoughts had changed. Being in the hole with all of that time to think curbed some of B.R.'s negative cravings. He still wanted to get money, he just wanted to do things a different way.

For the time being, B.R. just wanted to be home. He wanted to spend some quality time with Flower and he wondered what was up with Amiaya. Amiaya stopped writing him when he went to the hole because he'd always write her back telling her to go on with her life. After a while, she got tired and explained to him in a letter,

Look, nigga. If you keep talking that bullshit, a bitch gon' be gone when you get out. I know you're going through it, so am I. Just don't keep pushing me away like that. I'm gonna disregard all of that rhetoric that you've been kicking and I'm just gonna fall back until you get home. The most they can hold you is until your conditional release date, and that's right around the corner. I'll be here. I ain't going nowhere. In the meantime, know that I love you. Hold ya head and prepare to love me back. Okay boo. I sent you some books with this letter. 'Here Today, Gone Tomorrow' by some cat named J. Marcelle, 'Window Shopper' by Charles Threat, 'Street Kharma' by Dwayne Jones, 'Power of the Dollar' by Frank Tunstell, and one you should definitely like called 'Menage-A-Twist' by Michael Collins. I copped them from Walden's Bookstore downtown. Read more, stress less. You'll be home in a minute.
Love always,
Amiaya

B.R. remembered that letter because he read it almost everyday after he finished reading the books that she had sent to him. He only hoped that she wasn't tied down yet.

As B.R. neared the entrance of the building, he noticed twin BMW 740iL's parked back to back. One was money green, the other was candy apple red. Both had their windows rolled down with music escaping the interior like if inside the car a club was poppin' off. B.R. had on a wife beater, a pair of green sweatpants, a pair of beige Timbs and carried a garbage bag full of his personal belongings.

Somebody yelled, "Oh shit!" And the music in both cars shut off. "That's B.R." someone said unconvincingly.

"No it ain't. B.R. got 25." Someone else commented. B.R. smiled because people still remembered him. Then Hahmo and K.I. exited the building and spotted their boy.

Hahmo was on the phone with Cindy. K.I. had his lil man in his hands. Baby K.I. was 23 months old and looked just like his father.

B.R. walked into the open arms of his two crimey's and hugged them for what seemed like an eternity.

"What's up, Blood?" K.I. inquired. They gave each other some more dap and K.I. stepped back to examine his homie from head to toe. "You big as shit, kid." K.I. voiced.

B.R. kept his smile on display, happy to see that his family still had love for him.

Hahmo dapped his homie a second time, then embraced him with another big hug. "Damn kid, we missed the hell outta you."

"No doubt, no doubt." B.R. agreed. He knelt down to Baby K.I.'s height and started talking to the little baby. "So this is Baby Killer Instinct. Okay. What's up Lil man? Looking just like your pops." Baby K.I. clapped and smiled, showing the eight teeth that helped him eat chicken and rice every night.

B.R. stood up when Hahmo offered, "You want us to take you to Mt. V.? Moms saw you yet?"

"Nah, this the first place I touched down at. I pretty much got home, just now. You know I had to creep through and see what was up with the old stomping grounds."

"Shit is ah-ight. I mean me and K.I. holding it down, so you know you're good. Mad niggas got knocked or hit up since you been in and we only on like a joint and a half between the two of us. But we got dough. We just ain't have a reliable connect. And we got your 3rd at the crib." Hahmo smiled, referring to the brown bag full of money that they had for B.R.

"Damn, kid. I love the shit out of y'all niggas."

"Amiaya know you're home?" K.I. threw out there.

"Nah, what up wit' shorty, though? I ain't heard from her in a minute."

"We just seen her." Hahmo remembered. "Yo, you gotta see her. Shorty's a beast. She's doing her thing, too."

"What do you mean by that?"

"You'll see." Hahmo laughed.

Just then, a white drop top six serried BMW pulled up in front of 450 bumping Rick Ross' *Push It*. The coupe was sitting on four deep dish chrome, six star Asanti rims. The interior and the top, that was tucked into its hiding place, were powder blue. Amiaya hopped from behind the wheel while Cindy and Tia hopped out from the back and passenger seats. The three beautiful women strutted over looking like Destiny's Child. Amiaya didn't notice B.R. at first until he called her name.

"Amiaya." He shouted quietly.

Amiaya stopped, turned around and looked at B.R. "Rosevelt?" She asked just to make sure that she wasn't seeing things. The Rosevelt she knew wasn't that muscular nor did he look *that* good.

"Yeah, this is ya boy." He smiled.

Amiaya placed her hands over her mouth to keep it from falling to the ground. She looked different, too. No longer did she rock kiddie pigtails. Her hair was glossy and thick, so she always let it flow loosely down her back. Her chest was still big but her ass and thighs seemed to fatten up like a grown woman. Amiaya had on some white Rock & Republic jeans that were a stretch fit. The Baby Phat shirt she had on

121

fit her snug breasts tight and had *Married* stitched across the front in Rhinestones. She had on a pair of white Air Force One's that made her look like a big shipment of coke. With her hand still covering her mouth, her ring was in full view.

"Oh-my-God!" She said. She couldn't believe her eyes. Neither could B.R.

Cindy and Tia waved at B.R. He responded with his killer smile and a double nod, one for each lady.

"Come here, stupid." B.R. told Amiaya.

Amiaya walked over to him with her hands still over her mouth, crying up a storm and shaking like she had just seen Michael Jackson. "Tell me I ain't dreaming." She mumbled.

"Move your hands. Let me look at you."

Amiaya dropped her hands to her sides and kept staring at B.R. She was so struck that she couldn't move. B.R. walked up to her and inserted his tongue deep into her mouth. Hahmo, K.I., Cindy and Tia cheered them on as Amiaya finally regained her senses and returned the passionate kiss.

Out of nowhere, she pulled her face from his, wiped the saliva off her lips and uttered, "You gon' make me pee on myself, tasting all good." She hugged him again and tippy toed until her mouth was near his ear. B.R. bent down a little to accommodate her and smiled when she whispered into his ear, "I ain't never have sex before and I don't fuck wit' dildos. Make me cum tonight, daddy. Please. I need some dick in my life and I know you need some pussy."

B.R. raised up and asked, "Who's BM is this?"

Amiaya kept her eyes plastered to his, leaned her weight, smiled and answered, "Ours."

B.R. looked over at Hahmo and with his eyes asked him, *What's the deal?*

Hahmo mouthed, "I told you."

B.R. turned back around to face Amiaya and she suggested, "Hop in, nigga. I'll tell you all about it on our way to Mt. Vernon."

B.R. threw up the 'B' sign to his two homies, waved goodbye to Cindy and Tia and jumped up in the car with Amiaya. From the passenger seat, B.R. looked over at his woman and caught her winking at him. Then she mouthed, "I love you." And pulled off.

Chapter Seventeen

When Amiaya and B.R. pulled up in front of B.R.'s home in Mt. Vernon, Flower's Benz was in the driveway indicating her presence. Amiaya pulled behind Flower's Mercedes and parked. She killed the ignition, then hit a button that caused the soft blue leather top to come out of its back pack and close up shop. When Amiaya was about to exit, B.R. grabbed her hand and said, "Hold up. Let's chill for a minute."

Amiaya sensed an uneasiness about B.R. so she stuck her foot back into the car, closed the door, turned the radio on, on low, sat back and sighed. "What's wrong?" She asked him. She took his hand into hers and held it firmly.

B.R. looked over at the window of the great room and looking for some reassurance he asked, "Do you think moms is gonna be disappointed with me?"

"Flower? Come on now, Rosevelt. That woman loves you." She turned in her seat to face him. He repositioned himself and gave her his undivided attention. "Flower treaded those waters of the street life once or twice herself so she knows what's up. She ain't gon' be mad at you for going to jail. She'd be mad at you for going back. She knew what you were out there doing. She didn't like it, but she knew. If anything, she'd hope that you learned a thing or two from being away. You feel me? Even so Rosevelt, if push came to shove, she'd have your back in any choice you made."

"Yeah, well, I hope so."

"You'll be okay, trust me, boo." Amiaya smiled, leaned over and offered him her lips.

B.R. caught the signal, leaned into Amiaya and gave her a more passionate kiss than the one they shared in front of 450. When they pulled away he looked at her and shared, "I love you too, Amiaya." Then he reached for the handle on the door and added, "Time to face the music."

B.R. used Amiaya's key and tip toed into the house. They wanted to surprise Flower and just hoped that she didn't have any male company or wasn't prancing around the house in her birthday suit.

"Amiaya, is that you?" Flower called out from her office.

"Damn," B.R. mumbled. "How'd she know it was you?"

"She must've looked out the window and saw my car. I be out here almost every other day so it's not a big deal for me to just pop up." She whispered.

"You talking to me?" Flower spoke while tapping away on her computer.

"I was just saying that I was hungry and wanted to know if there was any food laying around." Amiaya was standing near the kitchen giggling because she felt funny lying to Flower. Flower was such an easy person to talk to that many people would come to her and make confessions. She was an advisor, not a priest so she'd tell people, "Just don't tell me if you killed anybody, 'cause I might go to the cops." She had once told a guy. She laughed it out when she said it to him but she was definitely half serious.

"I left a plate in the microwave for you. I figured you'd

probably stop by today since I haven't seen you in a couple of days. All you have to do is start the timer."

"No, you start the timer." B.R. said and stood in the doorway of Flower's bedroom office.

"Aaahh! My baby!" She screamed. Flower jumped up, knocking over the chair that she was sitting in and raced over to B.R. She hugged him tight, rocking back and forth and started crying. "My baby. Thank God you're home. Oh, thank you, Jesus. Thank you, thank you, thank you."

"Ahight, Ma." B.R. tried to pull away, but Flower kept her grip. She lost her baby once and would hold him like that forever if she had to.

"Don't *ahight, Ma* me."

B.R. started laughing while Amiaya was on the side crying.

When Flower finally released her grip, the tears still flowed as she stood there eyeing her baby. "Look at you." She cried.

B.R. was getting worked up himself and when Amiaya noticed it she jumped in, "Aunti Flower, Rosevelt was just telling me how much he missed you and how excited you would be once we got here."

"When did you get out honey?" Flower asked as they made their way to the living room to have a seat.

"I got out this morning."

"Then he snuck his butt over to the '9' where I bumped into him talking to Marvin and Melvin."

"The twins?" Flower asked.

"Yeah."

"How are they? How's their Aunt Bertha?"

"Ma, they ahight." B.R. answered.

Flower noticed how Amiaya was all over B.R. and how they seemed like they were up to something so she commented, "Use protection, 'cause we don't need no babies running around here messing with my china cabinet." She eyed them both.

B.R. and Amiaya sat there stuck on stupid.

"I can see it in y'all's face. Y'all didn't have to say anything." Flower said in regards to the, *How did she know?*, looks that the two lovebirds had on their face. "Y'all grown so I won't interfere. Rosevelt, don't hurt that girl."

"Ma, I ain't gonna,"

"Shut up boy and just listen sometimes."

"Ahight."

"Amiaya is special. She's also family. She's a good woman and even though I know she's not doing everything she's supposed to be doing and living by God's word, she's still a very sweet girl." Amiaya felt stupid because she thought that she was covering her tracks. "I love her like she's my very own so you take care of her. Now Rosevelt,"

"Give me another piece of chicken." B.R. interrupted Flower's speech as she prepared both of them a plate.

"You know I love you. And I will always love you. But one day you're gonna have to become a man and live by God's will as well. You're gonna have to leave the streets behind. I told you before that these crackas don't care who you are or how much money you have. If you violate their laws, you will go to jail. You just spent three years away from me. I need you home now. And it's obvious that Amiaya needs you home, too."

Amiaya blushed embarrassingly.

"I got you, Ma."

"Okay sweety. I'll leave you two alone now. I have to go to Staples anyway to buy some more ink and paper and stuff. If you need me, my number is programmed into the house phone. Call me. I shouldn't be gone but for maybe an hour and a half, maybe two. And don't be getting nasty in my room. Rosevelt, your room is still clean, thanks to Amiaya who's always sleeping in there."

"You've been through my stuff?" He asked her playfully.

"Our stuff, nigga." Amiaya answered.

"And stop using that "N" word around me." Flower scolded.

B.R. laughed at Amiaya because he told her the same thing time and time again.

"I'll see y'all later. Amiaya, do I have room to get out? You know you're always blocking me in."

"You ahight, Aunti."

"Alright now, see y'all later." Flower left the house, got into her car and pulled off.

"What now?" B.R. asked after he dug into his plate for another scoop.

Amiaya grabbed the plate from him and pulled him with her up to their bedroom. "You'll have plenty of time to eat later." When they reached the room, everything still looked the same except for maybe the brand new white Sean John down comforter that covered his king size bed.

Amiaya sat on the edge of the bed and kicked her sneakers off. She pulled her shirt over her head, stood up and went to unbutton her pants. "What you standing there for? Your mother said she's only giving us like an hour and a half and my ass is a virgin. It ain't gonna be no shoving and poking going on. I want it nice and gentle. So take your stuff off."

"Controlling aren't we?" B.R. said slipping out of his boots.

Amiaya was under the comforter, naked by the time B.R. was pulling off his boxers. When he placed his fingers in the waistband of his drawers, Amiaya's hands were nowhere in sight. She wasn't looking at his face either. She was looking at the opening in his shorts. B.R. decided to mess with her so he paused to see if she would take notice.

"What chu' waitin' on, Rosevelt?" Amiaya asked impatiently. She was thirsty. 17½ years of imagining what it would feel like that first time had her anxious. Her insides were wet and although she didn't mess with dildos, her fingers were very familiar with her soft spot. Amiaya laid there stroking herself while B.R. grew inside of his boxers. When he got fully erect, he stepped out of his underwear and looked at her.

"*Hell - - nah!*" Amiaya voiced. "That big o'l thang is not going to fit inside of this little coochie. I know, because all of my fingers can't even fit."

"I thought you said you didn't play with yourself." B.R. commented as he slid into the bed next to her.

Amiaya's eyes never left the snake between his legs. "I ain't say I ain't never play wit' myself. I said I ain't fuck wit' dildos." Amiaya looked at B.R.'s face. "How big *is* it?"

"I don't know." He rolled over and got on top of her.

"Wait." She pleaded.

"Wait for what, *gangstress?*"

"You ain't gon' eat it first?"

"Amiaya, you don't tell your man to eat you. You let *him,* do him. I know what I'm supposed to do. I was gonna kiss you, then lick my way down to your center. Stop being so hard and controlling. I got this."

"Ahight." Amiaya was still a little shook. She palmed his thing because she wanted to see how it felt. If it was as hard, fat and as long as it looked. She said, "Hold up," jumped out the bed, jogged over to the stereo, did something, then ran back and hopped into the bed. She smiled, "Finish where you was at."

Just then the music came on, *Let me lick you up and down, till you say stop. Let me play with your body baby, make you real hot. Let me do all the things ya want me to do. But tonight babe, I wanna get freaky with you...*

Amiaya started massaging B.R.'s manhood and it started feeling good to him. "Wouldn't I have spoiled the moment if I had asked you to suck it?" He spoke and moaned at the same time.

His fingers were talking to her clit so she moaned when she answered him back, "Rosevelt. That thing will not fit in my mouth."

"That big ass mouth?"

"Shut up, nigga." Amiaya smacked him playfully.

"Just chill, Ma." *Mmtwa* he kissed her. "Let me do me." *Mmtwa.*

When B.R. made it to Amiaya's center and turned into a kitten with a bowl of milk, he took all of the fight out of her. She was bucking and humping and pinching the shit out of her titties. After two nuts and a huge leg shaking orgasm, Amiaya returned the love. She closed her eyes and copied what she saw on the porno DVD that Cindy had loaned her. When B.R. started humping her mouth, Amiaya knew that he was about to cum. She pulled her mouth up off of him and climbed up until she was face to face with him. As he lay on his back he spoke softly to her, "You ready?"

"Mmm Hmm." She answered.

B.R. guided himself in while Amiaya wrapped her arms around his neck like if she were putting him in a frontward headlock.

"Oooh," Amiaya moaned when he entered her. "Oooh, oooh." She said as he stroked slowly upward.

After a while, B.R. was all up in her guts, pumping away. Both of them were loving it. Amiaya kept saying, "I love you, Rosevelt." Over and over in his ear. Then she got quiet when he sped up. She was holding her breath trying to handle everything that he was giving her. Then his rhythm changed pace. She knew that he was about to cum. She didn't care that they weren't using any protection. She wanted his baby whenever it happened. But before he came, she wanted to feel it from the back. Cindy and Tia would brag about the back shots they were getting every evening and every morning. "Rosevelt." She called out to him as he slammed into her.

"Hmm."

"Let's do it doggie."

When B.R. turned her over, he got the surprise of his life. On her lower back, taking up the entire width of her waist was a semi-large tattoo in beautiful script. *Black Rose's* was inked into her skin with a black rose on either side near her hips.

"Oh yeah?" He said as he prepared to slide into her.

She knew exactly what he was referring to. "I told you I'm all yours." She wiggled her butt. "And so is that." Then she arched her back, placed her elbows and face into the pillow and took her pounding like a trooper.

Chapter Eighteen

Amiaya and B. R. were sitting at a table in Amy Ruth's on 116th street and Lenox Avenue having a few drinks. They were waiting on their lunch, discussing life and all the perks that came along with it. All of a sudden, the topic of Amiaya's income became the focus of the conversation.

"Amiaya, you never told me *exactly* how you're doing your thing, *or* how you got hooked up. All I know is that you're doing big things, rocking ice and pushing drop coupes." B. R. had on a pair of grey LRG sweatpants, a grey long sleeve t-shirt, a white on white New Era Yankee fitted hat and a pair of low top grey on white S. Carters. A simple G-Shock adorned his wrist and he had about a stack in his pocket.

Amiaya had on the same outfit, minus the fitted and her sweats were peach. Her t-shirt was peach and had *Momma Meeya* written awkwardly across the front of it. Her S. Carters were white with a little bit of peach in them and she had one pant leg rolled up to her knee. In her belly button, Amiaya had an iced out navel ring that said *BR's* attached to her stomach. Around her ankle she rocked those same iced out initials and on a tennis bracelet on her wrist, also. She upgraded her Jacob to an iced out Rollie, and flooded it with pink diamonds. The studs in her ears looked like R Kelly's and the 30" Rose Gold Cuban she had around her neck didn't look strong enough to hold up the piece she had connected to it. Amiaya had a huge medallion hanging from her chain of one dozen roses, in Rose Gold. Each visible leaflet was smothered in black diamonds while the stems were covered in green ones. The wrapping paper that would have supported the flowers was dressed in white diamonds.

Amiaya had on a good quarter of a million in jewelry, she kept ten G's on her at all times and like the American Express, she never left home without the 9mm in her handbag.

"When you got bagged I already knew that niggas were gonna start acting funny. Some of your workers were getting slick out the mouth tryna push up and when I went around to collect, dudes was trying to give me shorts. I put the brakes on all of that immediately. I went and got a ratchet out of one of the spots where y'all keep all y'all guns at and just started stepping to niggas."

"By yourself?" B. R. asked. So far he was amused by what he was hearing because everything sounded surreal. However, stepping to dudes, especially a chick, sometimes wasn't always the best idea.

"Nah, I couldn't do it solo. I knew y'all had some gunners rolling with y'all so I went to the top. Hahmo and K.I. weren't writing you but I was and they knew it. What I did was, I wrote a letter to myself and pretended like you wrote it."

"Really?" B.R. crossed one leg over the other one to get a little more comfortable. Sometimes people had to get creative when they wanted something out of life, Amiaya was a sure representation of that.

She took a sip of her pink lemonade and continued,

"Hell yeah. I knew your word was like Pyrex, it held weight in the 'hood."

B. R. chuckled. Amiaya was too much.

"Wait, let me finish."

"Go ahead."

"So the letter was pretty much telling Hahmo and K.I. to back me up when I went to collect, so nothing would happen to me."

"Did dudes comply?"

"What!? I was like *B. R. said to get that to the house.* The next thing I know, I'm sitting on like $440,000. I was scared to death with all that loot. Then Hahmo and K.I. asked me was I also going to re-up for you. Mind you, I had no idea what reing-up meant, but I said 'Yeah' anyway."

B. R. smiled and shook his head.

"So check it, boo. I hollered at one of your workers on the side that I knew liked me. He told me what a re-up was and I knew I was not going to be buying any coke. But I had to do something. I was considered *that nigga* so I had to step up. I told everybody to give me a day or two and I'd figure something out. In those 48 hours that I was faking, all everybody did was smoke weed. A light went off in my head so I went to that same $200 a week lil nigga."

"Who the hell got paid two C-notes a week from my crew?" B. R. questioned.

"Ain't that what you paid all them lil young niggas?"

"Hell no! My lil mans and them got a nickel a week, every position, because I rotated everybody. That way nobody got burned out in the same location or shift. Also, none of my people would be recognizable to any cruisers driving the beat or any Narcs trying to cop because they'd switch up so often. But go on, finish *Mrs.* Queenpin."

"*Whatever.* So I go's and snatches up the young'n and I quiz him about the weed game. He told me about all kinds of trees but he kept stressing some shit called Haze, or Purple Haze. I asked him how good was it and he told me that he loved it. He said that everybody smoked it but that it cost too much."

"So you went and copped some Haze and here you are?" B. R. said it so nonchalantly because he thought that he had it all figured out.

"Actually, no. I figured I'd cop some Haze and make it affordable. Now how do I make it affordable and still make a profit? What I did was I copped one pound for $5,000 and bagged it up into decent sized dimes. I bagged up nine hundred dimes which came out to nine G's. I put the whole nine G's worth of work into shorty's hands and told him that it was yours and that you wanted $7,500 back. That lil nigga hit me with seven stacks in two days and the other nickel the day after that. Now I did the math all over again. Off of every pound, I'd make an extra $2,500, after taxes so to speak. So off of one hundred G's, I'd make a $50,000 profit. I realize now that either I'm a gambler, or I did the dumbest thing a drug dealer could do. I spent $100,000 my first run. One of your other workers that liked me helped me out too."

"And ain't none of those niggas want no pussy?" B. R. had on a face that said, '*Come on now, you had to give up something.*'

"Maybe they did want some ass, I don't know. What I am sure about is that these niggas out here fear you. Fuck the respect, fear lasts longer. They knew I was your girl and figured that this was your bread they were fucking with. They also were aware that Hahmo and K.I. would put fire to their asses if they played themselves. But you know what was their real incentive?"

"Nah, tell me."

"They wanted to get money. Niggas were starving once you left. They needed to eat. Niggas had habits, kids, some wanted to get fly, trick on bitches, hang out, you name it. So I fed them. They're making a stack and a half every time I give them a package and what they're carrying won't get them a heavy sentence. *And* I paid them in work. Move mine, then do whatever you want with yours. Feel me? So for a minute, I've been eating, *good.*" She gave a gratifying nod as if she were a genie.

"What's your profit looking like?"

"You mean how much am I spending?"

"Yeah."

"Not a dime."

"They fronting you?"

"500 pounds."

"How often?"

"Every six months."

"What do you have to give your connect?'

"Since I'm getting so much, I'm getting them for $3,000 a pound. I'm grossing nine from every pound. I don't sell any weight, all dimes. I got five spots that do twenty pounds a month. From each spot I see $7,500 per pound after paying everybody, so that's 150 stacks per spot. Monthly from everybody, I'm pulling in three quarters of a million and my people in Mexico City get 1.5 from me every six months."

B. R. had a huge smile on his face after doing the math.

"Don't get so excited though. This year was really like my first successful year because I took a lot of losses before I got things right. But now since you're home, it's time that I take a chill pill."

"So what your stash looking like?"

"I do take a month off every six months since everything actually moves in like five months. But after spending, treating myself, my moms. You know I bought my mom a brownstone in Brooklyn, right?"

"Nah, I ain't know."

"Yeah, she rents out three of the apartments."

"Damn, y'all balling."

"Nah, we aight though. But yo, your baby got us sitting on like 3 million." She cheesed.

"What!?"

"Yup, we good, boo."

The drug game was serious and the hounds were probably out and already on Amiaya's trail. Everyday in the 'hood people were killed for peanuts and pump faking. B.R. and his crew had had numerous shootouts trying to protect 450. Here it was, a broad, sitting on 7 figures, driving around in an $80,000 import with $250,000 in expensive African rocks wrapped around her body. Only one thing came with that kind of money, and it wasn't interest.

"What you trying to do with all of that money, boo?"

"I want to do a clothing line, Rosevelt."

"And you didn't think *one* million was enough?" He smiled with a tiny laugh and then he got serious. Life was short and having all of that illegal cash put you on the radar for either the Feds, or every hungry nigga around you.

"It was, but when you're in the mix, one meal ticket just isn't enough. We start justifying saying that we need to cop this for mom, or this 20 bedroom crib for us. And so on and so forth."

"Where do you call home anyway, Amiaya?"

"I got the crib that Flower moved out of."

"What!! You still living in the projects? Are you crazy?"

"Yeah, nigga. I ain't scuured. A bitch got heat." She flashed him the baby nine she had in her purse. "Did you have any other plans for us baby?" She asked B. R. seriously.

"Not really, but yeah."

"Like what?"

"I don't really know but I want to do something legit."

"Hold on," she told B.R. "Excuse me. Waiter."

A pretty Asian chick walked over to them and spoke excellent English. "May I help you?"

"Yeah. Let us get another large order of chicken wings and bring us two more large lemonades."

"Will that be all, ma'am?" The waitress asked as she wrote everything down on her little pad.

"You want anything specific?" Amiaya looked at B.R.

"How come you ordered some more food?"

"You said you had some ideas about how to get us out of the 'hood and keep us out."

"Yeah, but we have to put our heads together."

"So, Miss, could you get us a pen and a writing pad please?" Amiaya asked the lady.

"Yes, sure. Will this be all for the food?'

Amiaya said, "Listen, boo. We might as well put our heads together now and come up with something. I'm with whatever you're with. Let's just do it." She looked at her watch, it was still early. "We ain't got nothing but time."

"In that case, give us an order of green beans and yams along with that."

As the waitress added to the order, B.R. rubbed his stomach and looked at his baby. "I'ma need some carbs in me for all this."

Chapter Nineteen

Hahmo was just pulling his car onto 169th Street from Washington Avenue when a familiar face strolled out of the corner deli and caught his eye. Patricia, a twenty one year old, nice looking Puerto Rican chick, and the mother of two little boys from two different dudes, had on some spandex that had Hahmo horny. Her son Pito was four years old and Mark, his pops, was a nineteen year old black kid from Harlem that had three other children with three other women, all Puerto Rican. He was doing eight months in C-76 on Riker's Island for getting caught with a bundle of heroin that he was about to make disappear up his nose. Negro, Patricia's six year old, was dark skinned like a Dominican. His pop, Black, was forty years old, down in South Carolina doing a hundred years for killing a lady in a convenience store in a botched robbery.

Patricia lived by herself with her children and had no steady boyfriend. She was short, about 4'11", and had a little bit of baby fat around her tummy from giving birth to her two little sons. Her chest was small but she had an ass like most Spanish chicks had after having two or three kids. As far as her face was concerned, Patricia had a pair of lips on her that were unexplainable.

K.I. had told Hahmo that Patricia had some real good and real wet pussy. He said that it was so wet that he had to use a dry condom, pull out after a while, dry it off again, then resume pumping. K.I. said that on a scale of 1 to 10, that Patricia was an 8 in the sack all day but nobody he'd met, not even Tia, who he was madly in love with, had a head game like good ole Patty.

K.I. said that Patty was such an experienced head giver, that she could fall asleep with you in her mouth and still get you off.

Beep! Beep! Beep!

Hahmo honked his horn as he slid his Seven beside an old Acura Legend and double-parked in front of 450.

Patricia at first thought that it was K.I. who was calling her until Hahmo spoke up. Although Hahmo looked just like his sibling, their voices were very distinctive. K.I. sounded like L.L. where as Hahmo's voice was raspy like Jadakiss. Patricia was stunned that Hahmo was trying to get her attention because every time she'd see him on the street or near the building, he would never speak to her.

"Yo, Pat. Hold up." Hahmo shouted because she kept walking. He turned his car off, got out and closed the door.

Patricia stopped and began walking toward the street where Hahmo had his car parked. "What's up?" she asked him. She figured that he may have been looking for his brother and wondered if she knew where he was. Truth was, Patricia hadn't spoken to K.I. in almost a month. The last time they kicked it, K.I. woke up lying on his side, with cum all over the bed, and his dick sitting on her tongue.

"What's good, ma. I'm just saying hello." He told her.

"Oh, I'm chillin'. How about you?" Patricia was being

friendly because she was cool like that. Plus, Hahmo looked just as good as his brother. She also wore a smile on her face that many men had mistaken for an invitation.

"What you been up to? I ain't seen you in a while." He chatted as he walked up to her.

"I been chillin', just taking care of Negro and Pito." She wiped the hair out of her face that the wind kept blowing around.

"I usually see them with you. Your moms got them or something?" Hahmo was making conversation so that he could get her comfortable enough to approach her on some other shit. He knew she was fucking, she just wasn't smutted all the way out.

"Nah, since it's the weekend, both of them are with their grandmothers."

"So, are you busy right now?"

She could tell by the look in his eyes that he was up to something. "I was on my way upstairs to finish doing my laundry. Why, what's up?'

"Nah, I just copped some weed and wanted somebody to kick it with. You smoke?" Hahmo knew that she smoked. K.I. told him that all he needed was a blunt and he'd be smashing in no time.

Her eyes lit up. Patricia smoked everyday, whatever she could get her hands on and had two roaches up at the crib that she was about to break down and make something out of. "Hell yeah I smoke. What chu' got, some Hawaiian? Some Dro?"

"I got some Haze. You fuck wit' that Purple?"

"I had some of that shit like four times. Amiaya be hitting me off every time I see her. That shit is strong though. So I be selling half every time she bless me."

"You don't like it?"

"Hell yeah I like it. Some times I be needing the extra coupla' dollars."

"What up, you trying to rock?" He offered.

Patricia looked around. "I know you ain't smoking out here. You trying to get us locked up?" She rolled her eyes femininely.

Hahmo laughed. "Nah, ma. I ain't trying to smoke out here. I'm saying, what's up with your crib? Or you don't smoke up there?"

"Nigga please. That's my shit. I pay the bills up in that bitch."

"So let's roll."

"What about your car?"

"Oh yeah. Let me park up and I'll meet you upstairs. You know how to roll?"

"Like a pro."

"Huh." He said and tossed her a small brown bag that had loose buds and about six Phillies in it. "Roll up. I'll meet you at your crib in a minute."

When Hahmo opened up the door to his car, Patricia was still looking at him. "What?" He said when he looked over at her.

She placed one hand on her hip and asked, "Do you know what apartment I live in?"

He said, "Yeah, 4-B. Why?"

She smiled and said, "Let me find out." Then she walked into the building. Hahmo smiled with her, hopped in his ride and pulled off to go park.

When Hahmo arrived at Patricia's door, he knocked and turned the knob at the same time. Patricia was grabbing a few things off of the floor that her sons had scattered around but forgot to clean up. The living room was clean and looked like nobody was allowed in it. "I'm back here Mr. Hahmo."

Hahmo made his way to Patricia's room and sat on the chair that she had positioned so that it faced the T.V. "Whose chair is this?" Hahmo asked getting comfortable.

"That's my smoking chair. Sometimes when I'm by myself I throw on a movie, light up a nice joint and relax."

"What movies you got?'

"I have a lot of cartoons for the kids, but you might like this one." She had a DVD in her hand and was making her way to the T.V. "Did you see Madea's Family Reunion?"

"Nah. I heard it was crazy funny though."

"Wait till you get some of this up in you." She handed him four nicely rolled blunts and the bag that had the rest of the bud in it, along with the two other unopened cigars.

Hahmo grabbed a joint, lit it and inhaled. Then he passed it to her where she did the same and sat back on her bed.

Halfway into the movie, Patricia was riding Hahmo like a rodeo champ. Hahmo was laid back, massaging Patricia's tiny breasts while her waist did the pancake. The weed must have put Pat in overdrive because at some point, Hahmo rested his hands flat on the bed and let her do her. Her pussy was feeling *great* through the condom so Hahmo went against his better judgment.

"Oooh, yo Pat." He whispered as she bunny hopped up and down on him.

"Yeah Papi?" She must've been in a position where Hahmo was touching her spot because although she was on top, she was angled, and Hahmo was drilling somewhere near one of her side walls.

"You on birth control?"

"Mmm hmm."

"Hold up then."

Patricia stopped, then raised up letting his soaked member slip out and slap up against her sweaty butt cheeks. He pulled the condom off and showed it to her.

"Just drop it on the floor." She told him.

"Ahight, come on."

She slid him back into her and looked at his face. *I know my shit is the bomb*, she praised herself. She started off slowly at first, allowing Hahmo to swish around and enjoy the beautiful feeling of her gushy stuff. After he nutted and she felt him still hard as a rock, she leaned up on him, got back into her angled position and let him bring her to where she wanted to be.

"Mmmph." Hahmo was biting his bottom lip and had the ugly face on. *K.I. said her pussy was an eight.* "Oooh." He screamed quietly. She was still doing her and it was still feeling sensational. *Her shit is a 20 piece all day.* After another couple of minutes, she creamed all over his waist.

For a moment the couple just sat there and giggled, because Tyler Perry was a funny joker. "Where your bathroom at?" Hahmo asked her.

"Right there." She pointed at a door right outside her bedroom, and climbed up off of him.

When Hahmo re-entered the room, Patricia had her thongs on with a cutoff t-shirt covering her chest. He could tell she was self-conscious of herself because she kept her shirt on while they were sexing until he pulled it off. Now here she was, ass cheeks on blast but kept her upper body covered up.

"So you don't have a steady man?" Hahmo questioned her while passing her the blunt. Hahmo was feeling her sex game and was trying to pretty much lock something in for future thirst missions. He wanted to make sure that she didn't have any jealous niggas that was open off her because he didn't feel like shooting anybody over a broad.

She tapped some ashes from its tip then inserted the blunt into her mouth. She took a quick drag and shared, "I used to fuck with this kid from over on Tremont and Fulton Avenue, but that nigga's shit was too dangerous." She took another drag and killed the joint. "Light another one up." She said with smoke streaming out of her mouth.

"Dangerous? How?" Hahmo was high and when he got high, he got inquisitive. He wanted to know exactly what everyone around him was saying and he wanted to hear an answer to every question that was asked.

"That nigga had mad drugs in his house. He would always leave me there alone like I was his babysitter." The second joint was lit and she was on it like a true weed head.

"What he have, like a stash house where he kept his shit at?"

"Nah, the nigga lives there. He got a girl now though. I still see him from time to time 'cause he still doing his thing. He still be trying to get the ass, talking 'bout could he come over just to suck my pussy. Niggas know that can't no bitch get their pussy sucked without wanting some dick afterwards. And I ain't no dyke so I'm gonna want to fuck."

"So you ain't fucking him anymore?"

"Nah, I'm straight. I don't need the headaches from his bitch."

"I know a few dudes up that way. What's his name?"

"They call him Bullet."

"Oh, Black Bullet with the Infinity from building 1132?" Hahmo didn't know what building was in that area. He was trying to fish something up out of shorty.

"Bullet's from building 1469. He's the same one you're talking about though." Patricia was chiefing, trying to take the whole second blunt to the head.

"I know exactly who son is." Hahmo knew him. He didn't like him either. Bullet had said some slick shit way back to a chick that both of them were fucking. Hahmo let it slide because Bullet was ass, and before their conversation, a mere waste of time.

"Yeah, he got a lil dough. He's stupid though, because he keeps all of his money in a hole under his refrigerator."

Keep talking.

"He's a big fronting type of nigga. Always wanna show his girls his money and drugs. Then he thinks that the cops won't find all of his drugs that he hides inside of the broken air conditioner in his living room window. When you plug it up, it rattles, it just don't blow any air through."

"He lives on the second floor, right?"

"Nah, the first. 1-A."

That's all the information I needed.

"Come here for a minute." Hahmo told her with a weed smile on his face.

She bounced her way over to his side of the bed and said, "What?"

"Now that *I'm* fucking you, can I have some more?" He looked at the pussy print in her thong.

"Hell yeah." She went to pull her undies off but Hahmo stopped her.

"Nah, leave 'em on. Just pull them to the side." Hahmo beat the coochie up raw dog for round two in the missionary position. All he kept thinking about was *free money.*

Chapter Twenty

It was about eleven o'clock in the evening and B.R. found himself laying in the cut in a stolen Maxima on Fulton Avenue. Lil Hahmo and Lil K.I. were seated next to him and behind him, respectively, keeping their eye on the target. Bullet was in and out of his building, running back and forth like selling crack was a neighborhood watch job. *Niggas Bleed* by the Notorious B.I.G. was resonating quietly through the sound system because Hot 97 was dedicating their day to all of the fallen soldiers, male and female, of the industry. It was ironic that at *that* moment, Frank White told the trio what B.R. was silently thinking to himself. *We agreed to go in shootin' is silly, because niggas could be hiding in showers wit' Mac Millies.*

"Yo, B.R. I know you and Amiaya are trying to fall back and do y'alls legitimate thing but I knew you ain't like this nigga as much as I didn't. K.I. told me that you would've been heated if you couldn't get in on the action." The silence in the car had hovered a bit too long which caused Hahmo to convey his feelings. It was all good because it helped ease the tension.

"Good lookin', ya heard. Ain't nothing like a little rec

every now and then, especially on a bitch ass nigga." B.R. had been spending a lot of time with Amiaya, organizing and establishing the foundation they were gonna need to start their business. They had plans to simultaneously start a clothing line, sign artists to their record label, publish a slew of Street Lit Books and make straight to DVD B-movies from their titles. Working so much had placed a strain on B.R. so for him, a little jooks would break up the monotony in his life.

The important thing was to be focused. The trio decided not to smoke any weed because Bullet wasn't rolling by himself and they needed to be on point. Every time a fiend would pull up, a huge black dude about a half a foot shorter than Shaq, with a back as wide as the Nissan they were sitting in would retrieve the money and keep the customer with him. A second dude, almost as big, and lighter on the complexion, would hold Bullet down from the entrance of the building. Bullet kept his apartment door unlocked and would run in and out for whatever it was that the person needed. He told Patricia that all he kept on his person was $30 in singles in case a customer needed change, and would put the rest up in a shoebox in his living room. Whenever the money in the shoebox would exceed a 'G', he'd take the stack and put it with his stash under the refrigerator.

"Everybody remember the plan?" B.R. double-checked.

"Like the back of my hand." K.I. answered.

"Picture me being scared of a nigga that breathe the same air as me." Hahmo sang along with the song.

"There goes another fiend. Let's move!" B.R. ordered.

The three amigos walked quickly and quietly toward building 1469 with their guns by their sides. All three of them had on black sweatshirts, black jeans, and black Reebok

G-6's. When they got close enough, they pulled their ski masks down over their faces and stepped up their pace.

Juggernaut was leaning inside the window of a minivan that a customer had rolled up in. He was preoccupied playing with her titties so he didn't realize that he let his guard down. Becky, the customer, was white, 35 years old and had been married for ten years. She had three children and her husband, throughout the year, would work four months on the East Coast, four months in the Midwest and four months in Cali. Currently he was out west, working his ass off to pay the bills that kept his wife pretty, her implants puffy and her tummy tuck flat.

Big man had sexed Becky three times already, in the back seat of her Town and Country and was warming up for round four, when somebody interrupted his plans. K.I. walked up on him and put a .357 to his head while Hahmo, from the passenger's side, took the keys out of the ignition.

"Breathe too loud bitch and I'll put your brains on the nigger you talking to." Hahmo dug into her purse, pulled out her wallet and tossed it to K.I. "You good, homie?" He asked his twin.

"No question." K.I. assured his brother.

B.R. had the other big dude laying on the ground pulling his hands behind his back.

"Be right back." Hahmo told K. I.

"If anything out here looks funny, I'm shootin' him *and* her." K.I. looked at big man and Becky.

"If you shootin', then I'm shootin'." Hahmo told him.

"We can kill these niggas now, then."

Becky was shaking her head, crying, mouthing the words, 'No, don't kill me.'

"Big man, put these on and cuff yourself to the steering

wheel." After K.I. handed a pair of handcuffs to the Hulk, he looked over at the entrance of 1469 and saw B.R. hide on the side of the building. The smaller, other big dude was handcuffed with a thick piece of grey tape on his mouth, laying in the cut where the superintendant placed the garbage.

At the same time that big man was cuffing himself to the steering wheel, B.R. had swung around and placed his Desert Eagle up against Bullet's forehead. "You know what it is."

When K.I. figured that big man was secure, he pulled an aluminum bat that he had hidden earlier that day from under a car. He walked back over to big man, looked at Becky, opened her wallet and read her full name and address. "Becky McGerald. 716 West 62nd Street. Apartment – Penthouse. You live in a *Penthouse?*" He searched some more and pulled out three photos of her children. "These yo' kids?" K.I. was flipping through the pictures, then he stopped and showed them to her. "If you say anything about tonight, this is what's gonna happen to these ugly ass kids." The Hulk was being nosy so he was looking at K.I. *CRACK!* K.I. smashed The Thing in the face with the bat and broke everything from his chin to the bottom of his eyes. *CRACK! CRACK!* He hit big man two more times, causing his heavy body to slump up against the large Chrystler. Becky must've fainted because she was leaning over the passenger seat, awkwardly, like she was asleep.

Hahmo was in the apartment with B.R., beating the brakes off of Bullet. They already knew where the money and drugs were, but to make it look official, they jumped into Denzel Washington and Terrance Howard mode.

"Fuck is the dope at, nigga?" B.R. yelled after stinging Bullet on the top of his head with the ass of his gun.

Hahmo was running around the house, faking like he

was looking for something.

Bong! B.R. dinged Bullet again. "I said, where," *Bong!* "The fuck," *Bong!* "Is the shit at?" *Bong!*

"Yo, I got it!" Hahmo yelled from the kitchen. He pulled about twenty-six stacks from under dude's refrigerator and another $800 from the shoebox in the living room. He hit the air conditioner next and came off with 450 grams of powder and 1600 dimes slabbed up it tiny weed bags.

"Son, we up! We good!" Hahmo yelled out to B.R. B.R. didn't answer so Hahmo unholstered his cannon and slowly walked to the rear of the apartment.

"What the fuck happened?!" He asked his homie, shocked.

B.R. had blood everywhere. All over his clothes, the walls and the floor. Bullet's face was disfigured and he had a kitchen knife stuck up his ass. B.R. was standing over him, stuck in a daze. Hahmo knew where the behavior came from. B.R. had told him, K.I. and B.G., before B.G. got slumped, what happened to him growing up with Mr. Pervert. It explained his ruthlessness and psychotic thinking at times.

"Blood, we gotta get up outta here." Hahmo looked at B.R. B.R. still didn't move. "B.R.!! B.R.!!!"

"Stop screaming."

"We gotta roll. Come on."

"I'm coming. I'm thinking about something."

"You thi, nigga, let's go!" Hahmo pulled on him. After a second tug, B.R. fell in step.

On their way out of the building, K.I. had a smile on his face that they could see through his mask. With his eyes he asked Hahmo, *"We up?"*

Hahmo shook his head.

K.I. knew that look and that shake. He did it once before

when the four of them, including B.G. were at the Tunnel Night Club back in the days and B.R. caught his first body. Enroute to retrieve their vehicle, after a night of chilling and getting numbers, B.R. approached a white man that he said resembled his old foster pops. Without warning, B.R. grabbed the guy, choked him, pulled out his pocketknife and stabbed the poor dude to death.

Now Hahmo was shaking his head *again*.

Behind him, B.R. was walking out of the building like everything was all good. He made eye contact with K.I. and K.I. asked him, "You good homie?" Just to make sure that they were all cool.

B.R. said, "Oh shit. Hold up." Then he walked over to the smaller of the two big dudes and plugged him. *Blocka!* One to the head. The shot was loud as hell. Car alarms started going off and Becky woke up screaming.

When B.R. put the gun to her head, K.I. stopped him, "Nah, dog. Leave her be. Let's go, we out!"

B.R. had contacts in so the eyes that Becky was staring at were brown. And that's the only description that she was able to give to the police when they questioned her at the scene, in the back of the squad car and down at the station.

Back at the block, after they discarded their clothing, Hahmo asked B.R., "Homie, you want me to take you home?"

"Nah, call Amiaya and tell her to come and get me."

B.R. started walking off down Park Avenue. Hahmo was on the phone about to connect with Amiaya when he asked his man, "Where you gon' be at?"

"Walking."

Hahmo left it at that and simply relayed the message to Amiaya.

Chapter Twenty-One

Tito Puente's Seafood Restaurant

"You know I love you, right?" B.R. confessed to Amiaya.
"How much?" She flirted.

Amiaya and B.R. were on City Island Avenue, across the street from Neptune, celebrating over dinner. It was their one-year anniversary of being together as a couple, and from the start, they seemed destined to last. It was warm out that evening so B. R. rocked a cream Purple Label, linen short set by Ralph Lauren. The waves in his hair shined from the African Pride grease he applied earlier that morning and the Unforgivable cologne he dabbed on, had married women around him ready to cheat. His footwear was basic; black Alligator sandals with no socks.

Amiaya had on a white, backless Roberto Cavalli mini dress with a pair of matching Roberto Cavalli stilettos. Her hair was out, hanging long, shiny and fluffy, and she kept her jewels to a minimum. A tiny tennis bracelet decorated her wrist while her eyeball sized studs caught all the attention.

"This much." B.R. answered her and pulled out an envelope. He handed it to his sweetheart.

"What is it?" She asked him as she tore at the small package. B.R. just smiled at her and allowed her to investigate her surprise.

Amiaya pulled out the single piece of paper, unfolded it, read what is said and screamed. "Aaah! You got the marriage license!"

"Yeah, since you weren't making any progress with the preparation."

"I forgot."

"You forgot that you wanted to marry me?"

"No, stupid." She gave him her spoiled brat face. "I'm already wifey anyway, but I just hadn't given the ceremony aspect of it any thought. You know we've been busy handling all of our businesses."

"Aye, that reminds me." He began.

"Hold up," Amiaya said and signaled for the waiter.

B.R. motioned with his hands and face, *What's Up?*

Amiaya nodded her head softly and reassured him with her eyes, *Be easy.*

When the waiter arrived, Amiaya asked, "Is it okay if we could pay for our food now? We'd like to be on our way." Amiaya's smile could make anyone agree or disagree to something, depending on how she was working the conversation.

"Sure." The waiter smiled back. He tallied up their bill and handed her the receipt book. Amiaya and B.R. had a joint bank account so it didn't matter who paid for the food.

"Thank you. Be right back." The waiter said as he walked off with one of Amiaya's credit cards.

"What chu' up to boo?" B.R. questioned.

"Nuttin' honey." She mocked the commercial. "I just wanted to go for a walk outside with you, that's all."

154

"Well why didn't you just say so."

She rolled her eyes. "Gosh, can't a girl surprise her man sometimes too?"

"Here you are ma'am, sir." The waiter passed Amiaya back her credit card, gave them both a warm smile, turned and walked off.

When Amiaya and B.R. hit the boardwalk, they strolled in the opposite direction of where they parked. They were going to walk until they got tired, then hop in the whip and head down to Harlem.

"Isn't it beautiful?" Amiaya looked at her hubby. She slipped her arm around his, grabbed his hand and intertwined her fingers into his.

"What, the stars?" He asked looking toward the sky.

"That too, but I mean, us. We went from the projects, to the point we're at now. I remember borrowing sugar and bread from Aunti Flower back in the day. Even when you first moved in with her, my mom used to have to borrow money from a loan shark to help out when her check didn't come."

"You ever make grilled cheese out of that big block they give out down in the carriage room?" B.R. remembered his first year with Flower.

"With the free butter and honey?"

"Yeah." He chuckled.

"What? Couldn't no cheese mess with that." She couldn't lie.

"Damn Amiaya. I love your ass to death." B.R. said affectionately.

"Then why you ain't never give me the time of day until you came home?"

"Come on Miaya, you were too young."

"I was fifteen when you went to jail."

"You were fourteen, and I wasn't trying to get 28 for 14, feel me?" He said with a laugh.

She changed the subject. "So how do you like the Fall pieces for the Crystal Jordan line?"

"Everything you've designed or helped design has been really hot. I didn't realize that women were such a large percentage of our country's overall consumers."

"85%".

"When we look around us, the first things we see are cars and we figure that cars are mainly for men. But there are so many other things that can be purchased that we rarely notice."

"Like clothing." She reminded with a smile.

"You're exactly right. Like clothing."

"What about Amiaya Entertainment? You thought you were slick using my full name for every thing. Amiaya Crystal Jordan." She squeezed his hand tight.

"Let me find out." She added.

"I ain't think that I was slick. I wanted some ass." They laughed together. "You kept talking that 'I'm tired shit' all the time so I said, I know. I'll do this, that, and a third, name that this, and name that, that, then boom, I'm dick deep into the gushy."

"You nasty."

"No I ain't. I just happened to be born a man and men need the pleasures of their wives, everyday."

"You be tired sometimes too." She reminded him.

"When?"

They had circled the area and were now approaching Amiaya's BMW. "What about, *Fall back right now, Miaya, I have to finish editing this manuscript. Or Miaya, I'll meet you upstairs, this screen play is almost done."*

"And haven't I always made it up there?" He crossed his arms.

"Yeah, but..."

"But what?"

Amiaya was on the driver's side of her car about to let herself in while B.R. stood looking in the passenger window waiting for her to unlock his door.

"Yo, son. Son!" A dude tapped his homey.

"What?" Two dudes, parked across the street in front of Neptune, spotted B.R. and Amiaya.

"Ain't that o'l boy?"

"Who?"

"Look, next to that BM." The friend pointed with his head and a gesture of his lips.

Dude squinched his eyes to get a good look at B.R. and his female companion.

"I see him. " He confirmed.

"I'm holding son, you wit' it to get some get back?"

"I'm holding too." Dude flashed his man. "How did you know that that was son? I couldn't even remember dude. That shit was so long ago."

"Two and a half years ain't that long, son. And I never forget a face." Dude's friend revealed.

Over at the white BMW, B.R. was demonstrating with his sexy hip movements how he always gave Amiaya some loving, even when he was tired. Then he grabbed Amiaya, bear hugged her and swung her around with his tongue deep in her throat.

"You see the way he's swinging shorty around, that's how he was flinging those police." The friend also recollected.

"You down for a 187?" The main dude asked.

"It was yo' beef."

"Fuck it. We'll just take the car and remind him that he got caught slippin'."

"Bet."

When Amiaya and B.R. closed the doors behind themselves, Amiaya started the ignition, hit the button to push the top behind them and turned on the CD player. When they first pulled up, the couple was rocking along with Biggie from his first CD, *Ready to Die*. They were singing right along with him, every song, word for word. As soon as the music came on Amiaya pulled out of the parking spot and the happy couple resumed where they left off. Unfortunately, Christopher Wallace couldn't have done a better job preparing them for the worst. *Betcha Biggie won't slip, I got the Calleco wit' the Black Talons loaded in the clip.* As the song proceeded, B.R. subconsciously checked himself and realized that he had left his pistol on the table in the living room. *Touch my Chet-ta, feel my Baret-ta, buck! What I'm a hit chu' wit you muthafuckas betta duck.* When Amiaya got to the corner, she beeped her horn because the car in front of her took too long to move and they both missed the light.

"Fuckin' asshole." She mumbled.

B. R. was still rocking with Biggie Smalls.

Before anyone knew what was happening, two dudes, bare faced, exited a black, big body Chevy Blazer and ran up on the white BMW idling behind it.

The driver of the truck ran up on Amiaya and shouted at her. "Turn the car off, bitch! Turn the car off!"

B.R. was numb. He was heated that he would do something so careless. To forget his gun at home was crazy, which is why not a word escaped his mouth when the passenger, who he recognized, jumped on top of the hood, looked at him and smiled. The same way he smiled at him two and a half years before.

Dude had his gun pointed at B.R. through the windshield. *Boom! Boom!* He shot B.R. twice in one of his legs, then climbed over the cracked window, jumped on top of B.R. and started pummeling him with the gun. The other kid was having trouble with Amiaya because she was fighting back.

"Nigga, that's all you got!" Amiaya huffed and puffed. "You hit like a bitch!"

The dude on B.R. had already put his victim to sleep. When he heard Amiaya talking shit, he reached over and mopped Amiaya from the blindside. *Mop!* He hit her on the side of her head and sent her to bed, *early*. Both were dragged into the middle of the street while frightened witnesses looked on in horror. The dude who had the beef with B.R. jumped into the driver's seat of the white coupe and peeled off behind his homie in the big 4x4.

Once they reached the Whitestone movie theatre, the carjackers left the BM parked in front of the multiplex cinema running with the top down. He wiped it down for any finger prints that he may have left behind, hopped in the Blazer and got away.

Chapter Twenty-Two

Crackhead Darnell and crackhead Debbie were in the staircase of 450 between the fourth and fifth floors getting blizted. Hahmo and K.I. still had the building doing Verizon numbers and the work they got from Flaco had increased the recidivism customer rate by 50%.

"I'm telling you Debbie, you not gon' keep smokin' all my shit up all the gotdamn time and not puttin' out." Darnell was shaking and chewing on a plastic fork that he picked up off the floor.

Debbie had a stem in her mouth, feeding her lungs two tic tac sized rocks that she clipped off of a larger rock that she copped from in front of the building. Debbie was in her own world, somewhere on the Starship Enterprise. Darnell was beginning to look like a Kling-On and everything that came out of his mouth sounded foreign.

Darnell was preparing to take a hit from the stem he had in his hands when someone bumped him as they jogged past him up the steps. "Damn, nigga. You almost knocked my hit on the floor. Disrespectful muthafucka." Darnell snarled.

The dude kept on going, ignoring the mumbo jumbo that the crackhead was spewing at him.

Amiaya pulled up in front of 450 in a cab that she took from the hospital. She and B.R. were admitted to Jacobi Medical Center three days ago where the doctors treated her for her head injuries. She also suffered minor cuts and bruises from the tussling she had with the one car jacker. She was recovering rapidly from the mild concussion that occurred when she got smacked with the pistol, and was on her way to grab a few things that she had left behind in Flower's old apartment. The '9' was closer to the hospital than their Mt. Vernon home, plus she wanted to get the rest of her things out of the apartment before something happened to them.

She paid the African driver twenty dollars and grabbed her cane. She exited the cab, spoke to a few gentlemen who were posted up outside that she knew, and entered the building. As soon as she pressed the button alerting the elevator, the door opened and she stepped onto the conveyer.

B.R. was also doing good. The doctors successfully removed both slugs from his right thigh and he needed eight stitches above his hairline from when the other carjacker opened him up. The doctors told him that he couldn't be released until his MRI, Catscan, and X-ray results came back, and that could take up to a week. In the meantime, he and Amiaya hung out in his recovery room and played cards and the Playstation III that they hooked up to the television. Before she left to go pick up her things, B.R. asked her, "Why are you getting dressed?"

Before the movie they were watching had ended, Amiaya had excused herself and went to the restroom. After washing her hands, she exited the bathroom, still in her house shoes and slipped on her coat.

"I'll be right back. I want to run to the '9' real quick to pick up the last of my things." She walked over and kissed her man on the lips.

"I thought you *had* everything." He asked her.

"Nah, I left some things over there that weren't that important to me back then. But since this bullshit happened, I know we're going to be laying low for a while, healing before we decide to resurface again. I figured I'd slide through there real quick, grab the rest of my things, take a quick shower and grab us something from the Chinese restaurant. Plus I need some air. The air in this place smells funny. Like hydrocortisone."

"That might be these people's bed pans and stuff."

"Whatever it is, I need a break. So I'll be back in about two hours. You good, right?" She was half way out the door.

"Yeah, I'm ahight. I want a large chicken and broccoli and grab me an extra side of chicken wings."

"Four or eight?" Amiaya asked him. B.R. still had a couple of days to go and would more than likely want something else to eat.

He looked over at the microwave. "You think they gon' taste rubbery if I put them in the mic?"

"Nah, just don't put them in for too long."

"Get me eight then."

"Ahight. Love you." She blew him a kiss.

"Love you too. Aye! Hold up." He stopped her.

Amiaya poked her head back in, "Yeah?"

"If you see Hahmo or K.I., tell them I said good lookin' and that we appreciate them coming by."

"You said we. I'm glad you're getting used to saying, we." She smiled and left the room.

The six foot, two inch dude, prowling around the stair-cases in 450, stopped at the seventh floor when he heard the bell from the elevator ring. He peeked through the window and watched as Amiaya exited the mechanical metal box.

'Damn, shorty thick as a mug'. Dude thought to himself. He waited and watched her walk to her apartment. When Amiaya inserted her key into the lock, she opened the door. As soon as she flicked on the light, she felt something bump her and she fell to the floor from the impact.

The intruder slammed the door behind him and locked it. Amiaya turned over on her back to see what or who had pushed her to the ground, when a punch to the face increased the pain that was already dancing in her head. The concussion she experienced when her car got stolen hadn't healed. She was trying to defend herself but her head was killing her, making her feel weaker, which made it harder for her to fight.

Amiaya was kicking and swinging, while dude was trying his best to pin her down. At some point, dude managed to lean his heavy body on her legs, subduing her, and unbuttoned her jeans.

'This nigga trying to rape me'. Amiaya panicked.

All of a sudden, she felt herself being dragged by her pants until they were no longer on her. Her thong had ripped in the struggle so her bare ass cheeks and unshaven pussy were on front street.

The intruder dove on her and ripped her top, halfway off. Her Vicky's bra strap was too strong so it didn't pop when he pulled it. Dude was choking her, trying to remove the bra and unzip his pants at the same time. While they struggled, chairs and glass flower pots fell on the floor causing a small commotion. Dude had his dick out trying to insert it into Amiaya as she fought for dear life. He had her arms secured and her legs pried halfway open when the man above sent her an angel.

A neighbor had heard the ruckus and banged on the door. *Boom! Boom! Boom!* "What's going on!? Amiaya!" *Boom! Boom! Boom!*

"Aaah! Help!" She screamed.

The dude punched her in the head to slow her down. He got up, pulled out a .38 revolver and let off two shots at the front door. *Pop! Pop!* The neighbor ran into his own apartment and dialed 9-1-1. That's when the intruder made his get-away.

Amiaya lay on the floor, halfway violated and more angry than afraid.

Ring! "9-1-1 operator. How may I help you?"

"Yes, send cops to 450 East 169th Street, the seventh floor. 4-5-0, 169th. Seventh floor!" The neighbor hung up the phone and peeked through his peephole. He noticed Amiaya's door partially ajar so he called her name. "Amiaya! You in there?!"

"Yes." She cried out over her tears. "Help!" She managed to whisper. "Please, help me."

When the neighbor entered the apartment, Amiaya was laying in the fetal position with her ripped up clothing, barely covering her naked body. She was shaking uncontrollably, crying, holding onto her head and face.

The neighbor ran into one of the bedrooms and pulled a blanket off the bed. He ran back over to Amiaya and gently placed it over her. The old man cradled her into his arms to comfort her and did his best to reassure her situation.

"The cops on they way, Amiaya. It's okay. I'm Mr. Green, yo' neighbor. It's alright now. I knows yo' momma. I remembers you as a baby. You's safe now." He said in his uneducated, Alabaman accent.

He held her like that until the police arrived, then he let them do their job.

"You said you're her neighbor, a Mr. Langston Green?" The cop questioned him as he wrote down notes on his pad.

"Yes, sir. I's be Mr. Langston Green." Langston had his head down because he had always been a hard working, respectable individual.

"Would you mind coming down to the station with us and telling us all over again, what it was, exactly, that you remembered happening?"

"Yes sir. I can go talk to y'all at the station." Mr. Green looked over at Amiaya who still hadn't stopped crying, even as paramedics worked to strap her into a chair that had restraints attached to it. "Poor girl. I's was too late, sir. I's was too late."

Crackhead Darnell was in the house with crackhead Debbie enjoying a marvelous blowjob that she was administering. They were in the bedroom relaxing after smoking up $40 in dimes that they copped from one of Hahmo's workers.

When Debbie released Darnell's penis from out of her mouth, a little air got in somewhere and a muffled *pop* sound was heard. Her soppy lips were numb and black from sucking on the hot end of the stem on so many occasions. "You gonna fuck this pussy now?" She begged him while he sat back on the bed thinking about another hit.

"Where'd you get that from?" Debbie was referring to a twenty dollar bill that Darnell had in his hand folded and molded in the shape of a fake ring. Darnell was a dingy looking dude with a missing front tooth. It was true that he had money back in the day, but now crack was his best friend and he was satisfied with every dime that came his way.

"That son of a bitch who came zooming past us with the pink lips earlier. He dropped it when he was hopping down the stairs three at a time in a hurry or whatever."

"Do you know him? Are you gonna give it back to him?" She was stroking his manhood, trying to get it harder than it already was.

"I've seen the young fellow hanging around, but I don't know him." He laid the bill on the table beside him. "I think I'm gon' keep it. I'ma get a haircut tomorrow. I'm tired of these dreads." He commented as he rubbed his hands through his hair.

"Whatever you say daddy." Debbie said and slid her loose pussy down Darnell's long skinny shaft.

Chapter Twenty-Three

On the day that B.R. was released from the hospital, he went to a travel agency on the Grand Concourse and booked two flights out of the country. He and Amiaya were due for a vacation, so in the wee hours of the connecting morning, the couple hopped on a Red Eye and took it fourteen hours, west, to Hong Kong. The Continental Airlines flight 2007 was long, but comfortable.

Amiaya and her fiance' slept most of the flight. When one of them needed a break from snoozing, they would start a humble conversation with the other.

"How you doing, boo?" Amiaya would always begin. Although Amiaya was as tough as an ex-con, she was still a lady, and naturally more affectionate than B.R.

"I'm good, baby doll. How about you?" He almost always responded the same way.

"I'm okay."

At one time during the flight, B.R. had allowed Amiaya to sit on his lap, sideways, and just held her. The temporary pain he was feeling was more physical than psychological or emotional. Unlike Amiaya, B.R. was a man and built to last, so for the most part, he was good and would maintain that status throughout everything he'd go through. He caressed her and wiped the tears that kept forming in her eyes.

"I got you from now on, Miaya. I won't let anybody or anything, hurt you again. You hear me?" He turned her face to his. Amiaya had almost become a rape victim. The attempt alone shattered some of her protective barrier. She needed to feel secure, safeguarded, cared for and watched over. That understanding of love had to be strong and always present, and most of all, she needed to feel safe. B.R. provided her with all of those luxuries and vowed to give her even more from then on.

She looked into his green eyes and rubbed her hands gently over his waves. She kissed him softly, then pulled back and said, "You promise?"

"I promise." Then they hugged and she fell asleep right there on his lap.

Once they arrived at Hong Kong International Airport, they took a Turbojet ferry to the peninsula of Macau. Macau, Hong Kong's badass neighbor and rival to Bangkok, was home to multimillion dollar casinos, state of the art saunas staffed by nubile Asian geishas and strip bars where leggy Russian chicks practiced open political discussions on stage.

B.R. booked a suite in the Macau Tower for four days at $2,000 a night. When they arrived, it was early evening and they were starving. Instead of ordering room service, B.R. and Amiaya got dressed in a pair of matching Crystal Jordan short sets with Crystal Jordan flip flops and walked over to the Litoral restaurant. There they devoured the best giant shrimp that Asia had to offer for under sixty dollars.

After dinner, they went back to their room and cuddled under one another while watching a Jackie Chan movie with the volume on mute.

"Thank you, Rosevelt." Amiaya said and closed her eyes.

"Thank you for what?" B.R. asked her. He noticed that her eyes were closed and figured that she had quickly fallen asleep. He eased her from up under him, got up, turned the television off, turned on his LYFE CD, and slid back into bed.

"Thank you for allowing me into your life. Without you here, I have no reason to be here either. I love you, Rosevelt, and I always will." Her eyes remained closed while a smile decorated her face.

"I love you too."

Ten minutes later, they were sound asleep.

For the next few days, the couple just hung out and enjoyed the ideas of exploring the wanton pleasures of the small Asian country. They attended a Cabaret Show that was staffed by a bunch of Romanian and Russian blondes that put old school Vegas to shame.

They accidentally went to a nightclub called *Anything You Want*, that had deluxe private rooms where everything beyond their wildest imagination was on the menu.

"Come on, nigga. These bitches in here giving you the eye." Amiaya tugged on her man's arm.

"Come on, Miaya. They don't want the kid." He faked. He knew the broads were on him. He was tall, good looking, and was probably the only black dude in the city.

As soon as he opened his mouth, a tall slender Asian chick from the mainland walked up on him and stared openly at his crotch. "I said come on." Amiaya said with an attitude.

Amiaya had a little jealous streak on the low and B.R. liked it. As the two love birds cruised the streets sight seeing,

Amiaya decided to exercise an idea she came up with before they called it a night.

"Let's go in there." She pointed at the Jai Alai Show Palace.

"You serious?" B.R. asked her with a straight face. He wanted to smile, *hard,* because the Jai Alai was an upscale strip club.

"Come on." Amiaya smiled and escorted her date into the building.

The admission fee was zero, but there was a one drink minimum and the cheapest beverage on the menu was an $8 glass of tap water. Amiaya and B.R. ordered two Honeymoon Specials for an unknown price. When the bartender told them that they owed him four hundred dollars, B.R. said, "For what?"

Then Amiaya added, "We ordered drinks, not the lease to your damn business."

"Excuse me sir," B.R. interjected. "what exactly *is* a Honeymoon Special?"

The tiny Chinese guy looked around the club while B.R. and Amiaya eyed him. They looked around too, trying to see what he saw, but all they noticed was a cavernous black space filled with peroxide-blonde pixies from the former U.S.S.R., and a pole on the stage that was at least two stories tall. Then they returned their gaze back to the smiling man.

He sat the drinks down that came with the order and smiled at the American couple. He nodded at the beautiful ladies on the dance floor and with all the honesty in the world answered, "Whatever the hell you want."

B.R. smiled but Amiaya didn't.

"We outta here." She said and left the club

The couple returned to their room and Amiaya was pretending like she had an attitude.

She stormed into the bathroom while B.R. walked over near the bed and stripped down to his boxers. A second later Amiaya re-emerged from the restroom dressed like a stripper in fishnet stockings, a garter belt, stilettos and a Chinese face mask.

"Fuck outta here!" B.R. said surprised, with a Kool-Aid smile on his face.

Amiaya walked over to him ever so slowly and seductively, and danced around the bed. *MelSoulTree* was playing in the background, mellowing out the mood. Amiaya stood in front of him, removing what little garments she did have on, and when she got down to her stockings, B.R. stopped her.

"Leave those on." He got up rubbing his hands together and circled his girl twice. When he ended up behind her for the second time, he whispered, "Bend over." Into her ear.

She leaned over, about 90 degrees and held onto the bed. "All the way." He further ordered.

When Amiaya placed her face next to her shins, she looked between her legs and noticed B.R.'s boxers on the carpet behind him and his toes about an inch behind her heels. She smiled because she knew what he was up to and said, "Oooh." When he entered her. "Oooh, oooh, oooh, oooh. Don't stop." She wanted him to sex her forever. She loved B.R. for who he was. It had nothing to do with his money or status. As far as his sex game was concerned, he was incredible. So that was also a plus.

"Lift up boo, and place one of your feet on the bed."

"Like that?" She asked once in position. "Oooh." She moaned when he re-entered her.

"Oh, my, gosh." He uttered as he stroked away.

The couple made love all night and didn't stop until the

following day when room service told them that they had to change the sheets. After two young Asians freshened up the place, the couple ate and fucked like somebody was trying to get pregnant.

When it was time to leave, both Amiaya and B.R. were rejuvenated and feeling great.

"You ready to head back to the Rotten Apple?" B.R. asked his woman.

"Not really. " Amiaya said with a plastered frown.

"Me neither, but it's either now or never."

"Why can't it be never?" She asked him with her head pressed side ways up against his chest, while holding him very tight.

"I wish it could be, Amiaya. I really do." He raised her face to his and passionately fed her his tongue. They remained like that for a long while, then they caught the Turbojet ferry back to the airport. They boarded their flight and wondered what lied ahead of them once they arrived back in Queens, at LaGuardia Airport.

Chapter Twenty-Four

After returning from their trip to Hong Kong, Amiaya and B. R. stayed at home and spent some extra quality time together. Mrs. Berkowitz and Flower were at the house with Amiaya everyday for the first seven days, sharing stories, crying and joking with one another about everything. Mrs. Berkowitz was the oldest and wisest of the three of them but was a very humble and down to earth individual. She shared with Amiaya and Flower some of the horrific stories that she encountered over the years from some of the people she counseled.

One story, where an abusive dad would beat his son for almost anything, seemed totally unbelievable. The son's name was Trent, he was a junior, and his dad wanted him to grow up and be the baseball player that dad wasn't good enough to become. Trent senior had taken his ten year old along with him to a Yankee game where the Bronx Bombers defeated the Boston Red Sox 5 to 4. At the stadium everything was cool, Jeter did his thing, Giambi hit well, and father and son celebrated like true Yankee fans were supposed to do. On the ride home, daddy decided to give poor Junior a pop quiz about the game they just attended.

"Hey, stupid." Big Trent called out to Junior, who suddenly looked terrified. "I'm gonna ask you this one time, and you better get it right, or I'm gonna teach your little stupid ass a lesson."

Junior looked over at his father and wanted to cry but he knew that if a teardrop left his eye, he would have to ride home in the trunk next to the dirty old spare tire. Youngin held his composure and nodded, inviting the challenge. He knew that some consequence was inevitable because the question that was about to come his way, referred back to the game that he had not paid any attention to. Trent Jr. hated baseball, he wanted to be a football player and idolized Terrell Owens. Dad didn't want son to be a wide receiver, though, he wanted him to play short stop. For a while Trent Jr. figured, in life, sometimes you just have to fake it, to make it.

"Son, in what inning did David 'Big Papi' Ortiz steal second base and what was the error that Derek Jeter made which almost cost the game?" Father and son were driving down Webster Avenue, between Gunhill Road and East 233rd Street. It was a 2½ mile stretch of no stop lights or stop signs and big daddy was going 35 mph.

Trent Jr. looked up at his dad who was chewing a half pack of Big League bubble gum, that he didn't share.

'Dad looks like a horse with all that gum in his mouth.' He daydreamed.

"WHAT'S THE ANSWER, BOY!" Big Trent screamed.

"I don't know, daddy. I don't know, I'm sorry." Jr. confessed.

Without a second thought, dad reached over, opened the passenger side door and pushed his son into the street while the car was still in motion. Trent Jr. told Mrs. Berkowitz that he had to limp home because his dad told him to walk and follow behind the car. Two days later he found out that his leg was broken when he went to the school nurse complaining about sharp pains in his knee. The nurse asked him did he get hurt playing in the school's yard. Trent Jr. said, "No. I didn't know the answer to a question that my dad asked me so he pushed me out of the car."

"He did what? Pushed you out of a car? Was it moving?"

"Mmm hmm." Poor Trent answered.

By three o'clock that afternoon, Trent senior was in jail. Junior was lucky, he reported what was going on to a staff at school and was fortunately relieved of his situation. Many kids don't get that opportunity. They're afraid to tell an adult because they don't want to get beat *again*, for tattling. It's every adult's responsibility to be mindful of their children and the kids their children hang around with.

The story that brought Flower and Amiaya to tears was when a young lady, no older than twelve or thirteen years old, was escorted to Mrs. Berkowitz' office by a social worker.

Mrs. Berkowitz stopped what she was doing and observed the faces of both case manager Teadora Nunez and twelve year old Tawanna Smith. "Have a seat, Tawanna. Mrs. Berkowitz will speak with you now." Mrs. Berkowitz looked up at Mrs. Nunez who was holding her chest near her heart and mouthing, 'Poor baby'.

Mrs. Berkowitz applied that humble smile of hers to her warm face and calmly stated, "Tawanna, that's a pretty name."

Tawanna nodded as if to say, thank you.

"How old are you, Tawanna?" Tawanna hadn't taken a seat yet because apparently she wasn't quite comfortable around the strange lady.

"I'ma be twelve November 5th."

"That's right around the corner, sweety. Would you like to sit down, Tawanna?" Mrs. Berkowitz motioned with her hand to a seat right next to her desk.

Tawanna shook her head, no.

"Do you know why they brought you here?" Mrs. Berkowitz was almost always informed ahead of time about who would be coming to visit her, to give her time to prepare and strategize her interview. But every once in a while, a walk in would come through the door and Mrs. B would have to use what they taught her in school about being spontaneous.

Tawanna knew why she was there so she nodded.

"Go on, you can tell me. I'm a friend, I'm here to help." Mrs. B couldn't present her smile because little Tawanna started crying.

"I'm pregnant." Tawanna answered. "And I don't know who the daddy is." Her shoulders were jerking as her crying got stronger.

Mrs. Berkowitz had heard many horror stories before, so maintaining her professionalism wasn't a problem. "Were you raped?" she asked the child.

Tawanna shook her head.

"Who'd you have sex with?"

Her answer had a terrifying tremble to it. "My step daddy. My stepbrother, Tyrone. My stepbrother Mark and Mark's friend, Mike."

"Chile, come here." Mrs. B offered her arms. Tawanna jumped at the comfort and cried on Mrs. Berkowitz' shoulder for almost an hour.

Mrs. Berkowitz told Amiaya and Flower that Melvin, the stepfather, was doing twenty years in Attica. Tyrone, Mark and Mike all received fifteen years after losing trial, and were all spread out in different prisons in upstate New York.

Tawanna saved herself when she told her best friend at school that she wanted the sex to end. Her friend in turn told her mom, who in turn called the police. Tawanna aborted the baby and was able to continue going to school like a normal adolescent. She recently called Mrs. Berkowitz and told her that she earned a four year degree in Child Psychology and would hopefully get to save some other child's life like she had been saved. For the thirty minutes that they talked, the two laughed together and cried while sharing an emotional prayer over the phone. When they hung up, Mrs. Berkowitz smiled inside because the system had saved yet another one.

"I'm home!" B.R. came barging into the crib with three grocery bags full of snacks and dinner. When he entered the living room, watery eyes were everywhere. "Damn, I done walked in at the wrong time." He uttered quietly.

Amiaya laughed and said, "Shut up, stupid. Get in here."

B.R. walked over, hugged Mrs. Berkowitz, "Hey Mrs. B." Hugged and kissed Flower, "Hi mom." And kissed Amiaya on the lips. "What's up, boo?"

"Nothing. What you got for us?"

Mrs. B. and Flower were already in the bags unloading items.

"He's got some linguini noodles, chicken breasts, cheese, Ragu meat sauce, garlic. Bread for garlic bread, hmm." Mrs. B noted.

"No coolers?" Mrs. B looked at B.R. when Flower posed the question.

"Huh?" he answered.

"It ain't no coolers in here? Let me see." Flower fake searched the bag. "What are we supposed to drink with this meal?"

"What's the meal?" Amiaya jumped in.

"Chicken Parmesan." B.R. answered.

Then things got quiet. Mrs. B tapped one foot on the floor impatiently while Flower had her arms folded one over the other, across her chest. Amiaya stayed out of it.

"Ahight, I got something to tell y'all." B.R. boasted, with a smile that showed accomplishment.

"What?" Amiaya questioned.

"Tell us." Mrs. B chimed in.

"Yeah, boy. What you got for us? Some Liquor?" Everyone laughed at Flower's request.

"I got the deal for the community center and daycare attachment in Edenwald."

"For real?" Amiaya was proud of her man.

"Wow." Came Mrs. Berkowitz.

"So what's next?" Flower could also be all business sometimes. She knew what her son was trying to accomplish. Now she just had to give him all the support he needed to stay hopeful.

"Well, I know I need a few things. I already have it mapped out. The computers and stuff are gonna come from a wholesale recycling center at a Federal Prison Camp in Lewisburg, Pennsylvania called Unicor. I'll be able to get all of the electronics, computers, DVDs, T.V.s, camcorders, everything from there for dirt cheap. We'll buy the breakfast, lunch and dinner packs from the Arriola Corp. I know the chick Beissy who runs the place. Matter of fact, Amiaya introduced me to her before her company got big." B.R. winked at Amiaya's smile.

"There's nothing like networking. Amiaya Entertainment will provide all reading and writing materials and for any of the kids who don't really have any threads, they'll receive a care package full of Crystal Jordan clothing and Nike sneakers. Aunti Flora, we call her Lil Mama, 'cause she's so cool like that, but Flora will handle the distribution of the clothing because she's worked with the Salvation Army and FEMA with that whole Katrina thing. So that's another accomplishment for the Amiaya Entertainment Foundation."

"Wonderful job. So what's next?" Flower challenged. Her son was doing good for his community and she wanted him to keep the motivation that he had going.

"It doesn't matter, mom. The sky's the limit."

Chapter Twenty-Five

Amiaya was at the beauty salon on 116th Street and Eighth Avenue getting her hair touched up. She had on the basics, a pink Coogi sweatsuit with a pair of pink and white Gucci sneakers. Aside from her beautician, Sanovia, and 50 Cent's baby's mother Shanequa, Amiaya didn't know anyone else up in the spot. It was the weekend so the tiny place was packed with broads trying to get their do's washed, and set, permed and braided for the evening and the upcoming week.

Amiaya was there for a simple wash and set. Shanequa was under the dryer draped in some Lady G-Unit while constantly stepping out to chat on her cell phone. Occasionally she would type messages into her Sidekick but her phone wouldn't stop clicking. It was amazing how much information one could absorb sitting around a bunch of broads who loved to gossip and start rumors.

"Kim from St. Nick supposed to pregnant by Javan from her building." A fat chick named Tara told her girlfriend Trina, who was only there to see who persuaded who's boyfriend to cheat. Tara and Trina were from the Drew Hamilton Houses on 143rd Street and Eighth Avenue and knew everybody's business from Central Park to the Polo

Grounds.

"Get out of here. I thought they said Kim had the monster." Trina retorted.

"Her face do look skinnier now that you've mentioned it."

"So if she fuckin' Javan, and Javan fuckin' fat Monica, then Monica nasty ass got it too."

"Mmm hmm."

Two chairs down, a beautician and her client were also logged on to gossip.com.

"Girl, what you want done?" Liza, a thick Dominican girl from Washington Heights asked Moo Moo, one of her regulars from the Bronx.

Moo Moo was light skinned and used to be a dime back in the days before she had two kids and fell in love with a crackhead. Before she knew it, she was getting high but kept denying that she had a problem like Whitney did.

"Take my weave out." Moo Moo told Liza. "Make me look like Janet Jackson because I *am* about to lose all of this weight."

As Liza began her task, the conversation also began. "What's up with your cousin that used to come down here with you all the time?"

"Who, Dee?"

"I don't know his name. Is he the tall, slim, real dark dude that you said just came home from jail?"

"Yeah, that's Dee."

"Where he at, with his fine ass?"

"Back in jail."

"I thought you said he just came home?"

"He did –Oow! You pulling my real hair."

"My bad, sugar. You had this thing in too long. When was the last time I did your hair?"

"Last month on the first"

"You let this dag on weave stay in your hair for six weeks?"

"I ain't get my stamps till yesterday. I went to the Palestinians near my block and traded some of that shit in for cash."

"You ain't got a man no more, Moo Moo?" Liza loved rubbing it in whenever one of her customers either lost their man, or still hadn't found one.

"I thought you wanted to know about what was up with my cousin, Dee?"

"I do."

"Ahight then. Don't worry about who's fuckin' this pussy. As long as it ain't yo' man, you should be happy."

Liza leaned over and looked Moo Moo in her dingy looking face and informed, "Girl, if I ever, thought my man was cheating, you can bets believe that I wouldn't have to worry about it being with you."

"And what's that supposed to mean?" Moo Moo said and sucked her teeth.

Liza pulled up the apron that Moo Moo had protecting her from any hair chemicals, looked down at the beat up Reeboks she had on with a pair of faded Parasuco jeans and stated, "Not a damn thing, girl."

As the air got thicker, a familiar face entered the salon alerting Amiaya's antennas.

"You next, girl." Liza told Tanya. Tanya was a Puerto Rican chick that looked black and only fucked with abusive guys and dudes that where heavy set. She also lived around the corner from 450 on Washington Avenue.

When Moo Moo was done, she left with an attitude.

Liza said, "Whatever. I'll see yo' ass next month."

Tanya hopped up in the chair, told Liza what she wanted

done and shared some of the most valuable information she could ever reveal.

"How you doing, Tanya?"

"I'm good, ma."

"I ain't seen you in a while. What's good in the 'hood?"

"Pretty much the same o'l, same o'l."

"You still with o'l boy?"

"Who, Darius?" As far as Tanya knew, she had only told Liza about Darius, not her new man Kenny, which is why she was asking Liza if it were Darius that she remembered. Broads could be scandalous.

"Tall, brownskinned, kinda stocky with poppy eyes." Liza described.

"That's Darius. I ain't with o'l boy no more, uh uh. I been kicked him to the curb."

"What for, girl? Scoop me, sugar. Spill it out." Liza urged.

"That nasty ass nigga was fucking a bunch of crackheads and caught something. Then his nasty ass passed whatever he had on to me. Since Darius and I were having our ups and downs, like every relationship has", *Misery Loves Company* , "I messed around on him and gave my other friend whatever I had."

"And what happended?"

"He slapped the shit out of me and made me pay for his penicillin prescription."

"Drama, drama, drama."

"So me and Darius are done. My cousin's big dick boyfriend only let's me give him head, talkin' 'bout the only way he gone' hit it is if I let him fuck me up my ass."

"You fuckin' yo' cousin's man?"

"Hell yeah. She triflin' anyway."

"That shit hurts up the ass, Tanya. But after you get used

to it,"

"Please, I be riding that big dick every chance I get. " They laughed.

"So he's the new guy?"

"Nah, he's the guy I almost fucked up with, the new guy hasn't even had none yet. We ain't been no where, he ain't made no contributions to none of my bills, and he hasn't brought any food home. Fuck him. He's probably broke."

"And gay."

"And gay." Tanya added.

"You still live on Washington Avenue?" Liza asked her.

Tanya was only getting the back of her neck faded. The two news reporters were talking loud because they needed to be heard over the clippers.

"Yeah. My brother lives with me now."

"I know him?"

"I think so. He might've dropped me off here once or twice before."

"How he look?"

"Tall, kinda stocky 'cause he just came home from Riker's Island. Big pink lips and dark skinned like me."

Big Pink Lips.

"Oh, I know who you talkin' 'bout. Big pink lips."

Amiaya remembered o'l pink lips too. She knew he looked familiar but she thought that maybe he just looked like somebody she knew. Looking at Tanya, the two *did* look just alike.

"His ass is getting in trouble again. Every night he be coming in the house with all kinds of jewelry and lady's handbags and stuff."

"You think he robbing people?"

"I don't know. He told me that girls just be giving it up

to him. The jewelry, the money, everything."

"He better chill out before his ass get caught. And I don't mean by the cops, either."

"He need to. And it's the same thing *every single night*."

The last three words that Tanya let out seemed to drag and fortunately stuck with Amiaya like a bad habit. She got up and walked towards the front door.

"Amiaya, you leaving?" Sanovia called out. Amiaya was one of her favorite clients. She tipped well, kept her appointments and hardly ever put her business out on front street. Whatever she was doing, she was getting money, because the last time Amiaya came to get her hair done, she was pushing a white BMW. Outside behind 50's baby's mother's Benz, sat a white 4-door Bently Continental Flying Spur with Amiaya's name written all over it in off white paint. You could only see the writings if you were up close on it. Otherwise, the milky white luxury vehicle looked like the ordinary rich nigga's babygirl.

"I'm going to make a phone call. I'll be right outside."

"Okay, 'cause I'll be ready for you in like five minutes."

When Amiaya got outside, she called B.R.'s phone and he picked up on the first ring.

"Speak to me."

"Hey boo. What chu' doing?" She checked.

"I'm at the crib working out. Why, what's up?"

"I think I know who it was that tried to rape me."

B.R. got up and lowered the volume on the radio. "Do I know him?"

"I don't know, but I know you've seen him before."

"Where you at, still at the hair salon?"

"Yeah."

"You want me to come through?"

"Nah, I'll holla at you when I'm done."

"You ahight, though?"

"Yeah, I'm good."

"So I'll see you in a minute."

"You still ain't gonna agree with allowing me in on the action now that I know who he is?"

"Nope. You don't need that in your life. I'm the man, you just wear the shit out of your dress. Let me handle the husband's responsibilities."

"Whatever you say."

"What time am I gonna see you?"

"Give me like two hours."

"Where at?"

"I'm coming straight home."

"Ahight, love you."

"I love you, too."

Chapter Twenty-Six

To commemorate the ownership and re-opening of the daycare/community center in Edenwald, B.R. threw an Amiaya Entertainment party. The festivities took place at the old Limelight Nightclub located on 21st Street between 5th and 6th Avenues. E-mail invites went out to any and everybody who was somebody that had somewhere along the line participated in helping people or situations that were less fortunate than they were.

Kid Capri was on the one's and two's showing the crowd why he charged so much, while the jam packed dance floor showed him that he was worth every penny.

B.R., Hahmo and K.I. were already in the building showing hospitality, while the curvaceous and succulent hired hosts rubbed shoulders and mingled with all the special guests. Ki Toy, Esther Baxter, Buffy the Body, Hoopz and Mylissa Ford were all paid dearly to help make the event something to look forward to the following year.

The first group of ghetto celebs to arrive where the Don Diva family. Kevin Chiles, his wife Tiffany, Susan Hampstead and Cavario pulled up in a double black stretch Range Rover Sport. The black carpet was out so news crews, magazines, civilian bystanders and probably a few federal agents, were out in full effect, fighting for elbow room.

Kev stepped out holding Tiffany's hand with the help of a middle aged African chauffeur. Mr. Chiles was looking sharp in an all black double breasted Armani Collezioni two piece suit with a pair of black leather Burluti slip ons. *Mrs.* Don Diva was dressed gorgeously in a black shoulderless Dolce & Gabanna gown, Dolce & Gabanna ankle strap heels and a mini Dolce & Gabanna hand purse. Cavario had on a silver BCBG MaxAzria suit standing in a pair of lowcut black Salvator Ferragamos. Susan shut 'em down in a Gucci dress suit that stopped just above the knee. As soon as they stepped up to the door, B.R. showed his love and told them to go straight to V.I.P.

"What's good, Kev?" B.R. took Kev's hand into his and shook it firmly. "I appreciate you coming out. Hello Tiff." He nodded at Mrs. Chiles.

"Anytime Black. " Kev responded.

"Hey B.R." Tiffany greeted.

"Y'all got a spot up in V.I.P. Buffy or one of our many fine hosts will show you where it's all going down." B.R. smiled and waved his guests in.

"Cavario, what's poppin' homie?"

"You player. Doing it real big." They shook and half hugged one another when Cavario stepped into the vestibule.

"When am I gonna get my interview?" B.R. joked. He was referring to the Street Bible also known as Don Diva Magazine where Cavario did interviews.

"When you have something exclusive for me."

"Oh, I got something exclusive, alright."

"And what might that be?'

"You'll see when they escort you inside."

Cavario looked past B.R. and caught Ki Toy waving at him. On his way past he whispered in B.R.'s ear, "In that case, call me tomorrow."

The duo shared a laugh, gave each other dap one more time and Cavario met up with Miss ATL and found him a spot to chill.

When Susan walked up, B.R. gave her a welcoming tap kiss on the cheek and congratulated her, "You came a long way, Miss lady. Keep doing what it is that you do and you're gonna be around a long time."

"Thank you." Susan said and walked up in the spot.

Jay-Z pulled up next with Tah Tah behind the wheel of a navy blue Phantom. Rihanna and the Spanish cat Aztec, President of Roc-La Familia, pulled up behind them in a red Porsche Cayman and met up with the boss man by the door. Jay told B.R., "I been hearing a lot about you, young Cannon. When you're ready to take it to the next ten levels, give me a call." Jay handed him his card. Then he said, "I respect dudes like you. You have a lot of heart to do what you. There ain't too many people left cut from the same cloth as you and I. When you get some time, we need to make something happen."

"No doubt." B.R. said. And with that, Jay spun off.

Tah Tah had stopped and gave B.R. a hug. The two were cool and had met a while back when both were in a situation to prove their manhood. Back then, Tah Tah figured he'd give the youngin a pass while B.R., Hahmo and K.I. were thinking the same thing about the O.G. They bumped heads a few more times where they kicked it, hung out and formed a close relationship. B.R. laughed when Tah Tah walked up on him and worded, "You still got about ten more years before you can sip coffee with us." It was a private joke that only the two of them new the meaning of.

After a while, the spot started looking like the B.E.T. awards. G-Unit showed up about fifty dudes deep. Half of them were bodyguards. It wasn't like 50 Cent was pussy, he was still Boo Boo from South Jamaica. It's just that being in a very high tax bracket, you can attract certain circumstances. Young Buk and Yayo looked like they were on that lean. Banks was sober and probably on some ass from the time they pulled up. Mobb Deep looked like two little kids with a bunch of jewelry on and Mase was working the fans, *frontin'*. M.O.P. had their own party going on when a dude pulled up in a yellow Hummer H-2 blasting *'Ante Up'*.

By 1 a.m., Nelly, Nas, Rae and Ghost, Sharissa, Danity Kane, State Property, A.I., Marbury, Lebron, Carmelo, Chris Rock, Terror Squad, Superhead, Terrance Howard, Mariah, JD and Janet, Dj Clue?, Flipmode and a gang of others where 2500 deep up in the spot.

Buffy said her feet were hurting and took a chill pill over by A.I.'s table. K.I. and Hahmo were on Remy Ma and Christina Milian and weren't trying to give them any room to breathe.

B.R. was standing on a small bridge, over looking the crowd, beaming. He was happy where he was at. Amiaya was almost wifed up, Hahmo and K.I. were independent, Flower and Rosalyn were awaiting grandchildren and Black Rosevelt had upwards of 10 million dollars in cash and assets. He was a big boy, doing big boy things. He had K.I. and Hahmo on Pink Lips' trail and they said they knew exactly who dude was and where to find him. They also came up on Freaky Fo Sheezy's whereabouts after he bragged to an associate of theirs about the carjacking.

Free and AJ were walking by and they both had two

drinks a piece in their hands. "Aye, Free, you mind sharing?"

Free turned around and smiled at B.R. She had met him once on the street and assumed him to be another nigga trying to get into her pants. When they rendezvoused for lunch a week later, B.R. handed her a $50,000 check for her foundation and proclaimed "Amiaya Entertainment loves the kids."

"Where's Amiaya? I haven't seen her at all this evening." Free spoke genially.

B.R. gave AJ a pound and told Free, "She should've been here by now, but you know, *women.*"

She handed him one of the drinks and chided, "I do know us. Tell her to holla at a sistah when she shows up."

"I got you."

"Ahight, peace." AJ voiced.

"One." B.R. uttered to both of them.

"Hello Mr. Black Rose."

B. R. turned around and was caught off guard. Had he not looked the cream beauty up and down and noticed a body that didn't look normal, he would've thought that Vanessa Minillo had walked up on him. Whoever she was, she looked just like Vanessa, at least when she smiled. But Vanessa was skinny. This chick was holding. Mrs. Beautiful had on a brown dress skirt that had a split in it up to her hip bone. Either she had on a thong or o'l girl was free balling.

B.R. felt uncomfortable for a moment because he had never looked at another woman in a sexual way other than Amiaya. Now Mrs. "Kenya", which is who she introduced herself as, triggered something in B.R. that he thought never existed. Her hand was unbelievably soft when theirs connected and when she spoke, her breath smelled delicious.

"I'm B.R." he smiled.

"I know who you are." She blushed.

"You do? Well I know almost everybody down below and I personally sent out invitations to all of my friends and associates. For some reason, I don't recall meeting someone as beautiful as yourself, *anytime* in my life."

Kenya smiled warmly and patted B.R. on his hand. She was real feminine and as sexy as any model. "Maybe you've just seen me around." She flirted.

"Maybe."

They continued their conversation and as they got better acquainted, Amiaya entered the building.

"You seen my husband?" Amiaya was filled with delight when she noticed all of the people in attendance. "Hey, Remy." She waved at the Terror Squad Queen.

Remy waved back as Hahmo responded. "Son is around here somewhere. Give him a minute, he'll pop up."

"Ahight."

As soon as Amiaya turned around, Missy Elliot and Lil Kim walked up on her, "Hey, girl." They embraced.

"So you're with PETA. I guess you're about to throw paint on my coat or something."

"Actually, no." Kenya told B.R. "I'm just here to find out why a handsome man such as yourself, who is doing so much for his community, would condone the harming of these animals."

B.R. chuckled because Kenya was still beautiful even though she had become serious. She was on B.R. from the moment he pulled up in a floor length silver and white Siberian puma. *Rare* was being modest when describing this beautiful animal, extinct was more like it. The animal's head served as the hood. "Look, Miss PETA. I have no idea how the process goes when it comes to skinning animals and making beautiful clothing out of them. I just know that they cost an arm, head, and a leg." B.R. was bugging that Kenya had approached him on some next shit but he kept things cool and professional.

While they were talking, Amiaya, as she conducted her search, spotted the two huddled together, up in the cut, alone. B.R. was smiling, so something had him happy. O'l girl was blushing which meant that she was feeling good, too.

"Fur is an animal's skin. People sometimes never pay attention to even their own. Do you?"

"Of course I do." B.R. told her. He thought that she meant like cleansing it or something.

"Let me see." She touched his face and it tickled so he smiled, but he held in his laugh. "Nice. " She commented.

"Do you take care of yours?" He asked her.

"I have a little fur on mine." She informed.

Amiaya hadn't blinked since o'l girl rubbed her man's face.

"You want to see it?"

B.R. was so close to her that it looked like he was about to kiss her. If only he could see Amiaya's face.

"I can't, really," He said trying desperately to locate her facial hairs.

"Touch it." She offered and placed B.R.'s hand on her cheek. She guided his palm over her jaw and chin. "Can't you feel it?"

Amiaya was like a demon possessed as she made her way up to the bridge level of the club.

"That's a female's beard. That ain't fur." He laughed.

"Regardless. It's my skin and I should be able to keep it. Call me when you want to help us put an end to all of this,

AAAH!"

Amiaya yanked Kenya by her hair before B.R. had a chance to grab her business card. B.R. was shocked. *Fuck Amiaya come from?*

He jumped between Amiaya and Kenya but Amiaya wouldn't release the grip she had on Kenya's hair.

"Amiaya, what the!"

"Fuck you, nigga!" She released one of the hands she had on Kenya and caught B.R. flush on the cheek with an open hand punch. *Pap!*

Then she swung down and popped Kenya on the nose causing her to bleed.

"Oh shit! Amiaya, if you don't, uh-uh, come here!" B.R. was struggling with Amiaya. Hahmo and K.I. had come to the rescue when Amiaya brushed past them in a hurry. As soon as she grabbed Kenya, they made their way upstairs.

There were empty rooms on the upper level and B.R. had drug Amiaya into one of them before anyone downstairs knew what happened.

"Make sure shorty's ahight." B.R. told Hahmo, referring to Kenya. He was doing too well and didn't need any negative press or lawsuits coming at him anytime soon.

"*Make sure shorty's ahight*?!" Amiaya repeated. She figured B.R. to be on the other girl's side. "Get off me!" She fought until her shirt was almost over her head.

B.R. bear hugged her and ordered her to calm down.

"You want me to calm down? Huh? Calm me down, nigga! You all up in bitches' faces touching them and shit. Get off me! Get, the fuck, off me!" Amiaya was still twisted up, half crying, in B.R.'s arms.

"Fine then!" B.R. released her and just stood there staring at her. Amiaya was crying and was trying to fix her clothing.

"It wasn't what you thought it was." B.R. was calming down.

"FUCK YOU!"

"Amiaya."

"Fuck! You!" She yelled again while she rebuttoned her blouse.

"You know what, I have over 2,000 guests downstairs that came out to show us some love, and here you are acting crazy."

"I'll show you crazy. And I don't give a fuck how many muthafuckas are down there. Let me see that bitch outside." Amiaya was on her way out. "Don't touch me!" she brushed his hand off hers.

"I won't then. When you calm your ass down, then I'll talk to you."

"I don't know how you're gonna do that, 'cause I ain't gonna be home." She was on her way out the door.

"Oh yeah. Don't be home when I get there! Watch what happens!" Truth be told, B.R. had no idea what he would do if Amiaya weren't home when he got there later on. He never put his hands on her and didn't plan to. She was his life.

"I won't. And you ain't gon' do shit!" She yelled behind her.

"Fuck this," B.R. lunged at her to grab her and when she noticed the fire in his eyes, she ran. She jogged all the way out of the club, hopped in her Bentley and peeled off.

B.R. stood on the small bridge alone, observing everyone enjoying themselves. "Damn." Was all he could say.

Chapter Twenty-Seven

When B.R. entered his home at around 5:30 the next morning, Amiaya was sitting in the living room talking on the telephone. A bowl of Chunky Munky flavored ice cream from Ben and Jerry's that she had resting on her lap was almost gone and the television was muted on MTV. Nick Cannon and crew were Wild 'N' Out while Amiaya was stuffing her face.

B.R. walked past Amiaya without acknowledging her and heard her say, "He can't even look me in my face."

He jogged up the steps and was doing something on the upper level of their home for about five minutes. When he came back down, Amiaya stopped in the middle of her sentence because B.R. was butt ass naked except for the tie he had around his neck and the fur coat that had initially caused the rift between them.

He changed the channel from MTV to B.E.T. where Beyonce was shaking the hell out of what her mama gave her. He stayed staring at the video for about 45 seconds, then he flipped the channel to MTV 2, right after giving Amiaya an uncomfortable stare.

"I think this nigga is about to trip." Amiaya whispered

into the phone.

T.I. had a bunch of sexy video vixens trying their best to grab his attention in his new video. B.R. watched Tip's mini movie all the way through since the self proclaimed King of the South was on his last verse. He then popped in a porno DVD where Superhead and Mr. Marcus fucked and sucked like they were in love with one another. He observed as Ms. Steffans did what she was born to do. After a few minutes of watching some professional fellatio going on, B.R. ejected the Superhead DVD and inserted one of him and Amiaya getting busy.

On the large, flat screen, B.R. had his tongue so far up Amiaya's pussy that it looked like he was trying to lick the under side of her navel. As he watched the tube, his manhood started stiffening up.

Amiaya was on the phone, quiet.

"What's going on, girl?" her nosy friend asked her.

"I'll call you back." Amiaya snuck and hung up the phone.

When Amiaya's on screen character reached her peak, B.R. was as hard as a G.E.D. test. He looked over at his fiancé and noticed her nipples, pressed up against her tight t-shirt, waiting to be twisted and turned. B.R. had the serious face on and spoke rather calmly although he was very upset. "My shit don't get hard for no other woman except you, Amiaya."

She bit down on her lip to block her smile.

"You see this coat," He removed the Puma from his body and draped it over his arm. His dick was still growing. "That broad that you saw was down with the people from PETA. She made a complaint about my coat, but did it in a manner where it was more subtle than wilding out and throwing paint on a nigga's shit. She then tried to illustrate a point where she made mention about us having skin, just like animals, and used her hands to make her point."

Aimaya still hadn't opened her mouth because her mother, Flower *and* Mrs. Berkowitz, always told her that when a man was trying to explain himself, to hear him out. Because if you cut him off, you might not ever get another opportunity at finding out what it was that he had on his mind. "I don't know that lady, I don't like that lady and I'm not messing around with that lady. I only have enough room in my heart for one person and that's you, Amiaya."

B.R. was breathing semi-hard because he was upset with his girl and her jealous behavior. Amiaya couldn't even hide it. She believed her man and showed him by taking off her t-shirt. "Come here." She told him as she eased out of her sweats and panties. B.R. stood in front of her and Amiaya grabbed the head of his penis. She kept her eyes focused on his and spoke into his Johnson like it was a microphone. "I'm sorry daddy." Then she blew on it as if she were trying give it a sound check. That did it. The ice was broken and B.R. was halfway down her throat.

The couple stayed like that for a while and when B.R. felt himself about to cum, he tried to pull back but Amiaya said, "Um-mm." And kept him inside her mouth.

That was the first time B.R. left some babies in Amiaya's throat. She swallowed every drop and kept on going without missing an adlib. When her mouth got tired, Amiaya leaned back and spread her legs apart in a position that made her look double jointed. Slowly, B.R. entered her. Before long he was deep dicking her fast and hard. Amiaya had tears streaming down her cheeks because this time the sex felt different. It was always good, but for some reason, this love seemed more passionate.

B.R. slowed his pace up and gave her long, slow strokes.

He wasn't cumming again anytime soon so Amiaya sat back and enjoyed the ride. He pulled himself out, looked at it glistening, then slid damn near a foot back up into her. He repeated what he was doing about four times, then went back to pounding her. After another ten minutes he pulled out again, looked at it, put it back in, but this time only gave short, two inch strokes.

Amiaya was rubbing her clit uncontrollably while B.R. played with her emotions. The whole time they made love, not a sound left his mouth. When he figured he'd stop teasing, he pulled her down onto the plush carpet, then lifted her up and slid her onto his coat. She tried to get on all fours but B.R. pushed her back on her back. He opened her legs, slid himself all the way in, then he closed her legs together and slid them under him. He was on top, fucking her missionary with her legs clamped around his shaft. She was getting the best of both worlds. Her pussy was getting fed and her clit was getting the massage of its life. As soon as she began her first of a series of orgasms, B.R. finally said something. "This is what I think about that broad from PETA." He picked up his pace again. "Fuck her!", he said. Amiaya exploded but B.R. kept going. He kept going until she exploded about three more times then he released himself all up in her.

When he peeled himself from between his woman's legs he warned, "Don't ever underestimate the love that I have for you, unless you underestimate the love you have for yourself."

Amiaya just laid there, smiling. B.R. got up and headed to the second floor. "I hope you got your dress 'cause we get married in 30 days." He yelled from upstairs. He then closed the door to the bathroom. A minute later the shower came on and Amiaya fell asleep dreaming about walking down the aisle.

Chapter Twenty-Eight

It was about 11:30 p.m. when Hahmo exited 450, turned right and walked toward the small delicatessen on the corner of Washington Avenue. K.I. was coming *from* the direction of the bodega, strolling quietly behind Pink Lips. When the team sandwiched him in, Hahmo had a baby nine drawn down by his hip and expressed, "Playboy, we need to holla at you in the building."

Pink Lips turned to run and thought that he was looking into a mirror when he bumped into K.I. Killer Instinct was on him, pointing a .380 at his stomach that looked like a tinier 9mm.

"What I do?" Pink Lips pleaded with his hands up.

"We about to find out." Hahmo said and grabbed him by his sweater.

When the trio entered the building, B.R. was holding the elevator for them. They entered the conveyor, the door closed and for the twenty seconds that the lights blinked out, they beat the snot out of o'l boy. The elevator stopped on the seventh floor where the four of them exited and walked toward Flower's old apartment.

"Remember this crib, homie?" B.R. rammed Pink Lips'

head into the door and it almost knocked him out. He opened the door and forced Pink Lips to a back room that was empty except for a chair that sat in the middle of the floor, nailed to the ground. B.R. swung and punched Pink Lips on the top of his nose. *Blop!* Pinky went down, he was out for the count. When he woke up, he was butter balled, strapped down to the chair with a Heineken bottle shoved up his ass. After focusing a little, Pinky noticed B.R. reaching for an iron that was plugged into the wall.

Lips was Puerto Rican and when he first got snatched up, he tried that *'Mirra, Mirra. Me no speaky no English'*, shit but it didn't work. Now he had a handkerchief in his mouth with a piece of tape covering the cloth. All he could do was hum. The first time the iron touched him, Pinky squealed and tried desperately to shake his way free. B.R. pulled the hot metal up off of him and let Hahmo douse dude with some hot water. As soon as the water hit him, K. I. started swinging the buckle end of a leather belt on the spot that had been burned. After blackening and peeling dude's whole back off, the trio tried something different.

B.R. took a single edged razor blade, grabbed dude's hand and placed the razor under the captive's finger nail. Pinky's head wasn't strapped so when he felt the incision, he started jerking his neck motioning, "No", real fast and aggressive. That was B.R.'s signal to start digging. He cut off all of Pinky's nails and pulled on any remaining skin that was still attached to it.

Next they tightened o'l boy's legs that were strapped to the legs on the chair so dude couldn't move them. Pinky's eyes were shut but he was still breathing. K.I. re-entered the room with a large hammer and handed it to B.R. Black Rose knelt down low enough to reach the boy's feet, and started hammering on Pink Lips' toes. He kept banging until they were flat pieces of bloody flesh. The kid was crying and trying his best to scream but the handkerchief prevented any audible sounds from escaping.

When B.R. got up, he used the handle part of the same hammer and popped dude on the side of his head. He didn't hit him too hard, just enough to daze the joker. Hahmo and K.I. untied Pinky's hands and feet but left his mouth muffled. When the restraints were unloosened, Lips fell to the ground. B.R. hopped on his back and used the hammer to shatter the Hieneken that was all the way up his ass. The kid stiffened up and watched as K.I. and Hahmo left the room. B.R. walked over to the window and opened it. Then he walked next to a closet in the room and kicked it. Something was heard rustling around inside, then all of a sudden B.R. opened the door to the closet and ran out of the room.

He locked the door from the outside and ran to the bedroom beside the one o'l boy was in. Once in the other room, he stuck his head out the window. The apartment was facing the back of the building. B.R. looked to his left, saw the window still open of the room that Pink Lips was in and looked further to his left at Hahmo and K.I. They were also hanging halfway out of their windows. About a minute later, Pink Lips hit the window but was pulled back in by the angry pit bull that was hidden in the closet. On his second try, Lips made it to the ledge, climbed out on the windowsill, looked back at the raging dog, hung from the bars and jumped to his death.

The trio stuffed their heads back into the apartment and closed the windows while B.R. pulled out his cell phone. He called up his homie.

Ring!

"Dogman here."

"I got something for you to clean up." B.R. worded.

"Where you at?"

"Two floors down."

"See you in two mics."

Click!

•   •   •

"You think this nigga gonna be up in there?" B.R. checked with Hahmo.

"My sources tell me that homie be up in the spot every Tuesday."

"Ha! My *sources*." K.I. chuckled at the terminology that Hahmo just used.

"They be patting niggas down at the door?" B.R. asked.

"Do they." Hahmo and K.I. answered simultaneously.

"Fuck it. I'ma be outside in the cut anyway. Get him to leave the building and I got it from there."

"Gotcha'." Hahmo agreed.

K.I. reached over, raised the volume on the radio and allowed Young Buk to gas his head up. *'Every time you take a look at the news, we on the front page/and we in the Bahamas wit' A.K.s on the stage. The ice in the Jacob watch' LL make a broke nigga hate something, but you know I keep the 4-5th with no safety button...'*

The trio was in a newer model Dodge Durango with New Jersey plates on it. Hahmo had stolen the truck from the parking lot of the Bay Plaza shopping center in Co-Op City. Parked next to it was an older model Dodge with Jersey tags attached to the front and back bumpers. K.I. removed the plate from the front bumper and hopped in the 4x4 with Hahmo as soon as he got it started. They parked it in the

Pathmark parking lot on Third Avenue in Mt. Vernon, went back later on that evening after taking care of Pink Lips and headed down the block to Sue's Rendezvous.

"You want to park up on Lincoln?" Hahmo double checked as they neared the location.

"Nah, make the right on Gramaton Ave., pull a little bit past the entrance and you'll see a parking lot. Drive up in there first to see if this nigga's Lincoln LS is parked out there."

"No doubt."

When the trio reached Gramaton from Lincoln Avenue, they made a right and spotted the club's neon lights in the middle of the block. Hahmo continued on slowly and spotted an orange Lamborgini parked directly in front of Sue's with Ferrari rims on it. Behind it was an identical Lambo, but this one was black. "That's Busta's orange Diablo right there. He stay up in here too."

"Who the black one belong to?" B.R. asked.

"Swizz Beats. You know them niggas live around here somewhere."

"Damn, who the fuck are those niggas?" B.R. was looking at two huge black dudes posted up in front of the club with black muscle shirts on that had *Sue's* written across the chest.

"Those are the security for the spot. There's two more big niggas that look just like them, waiting inside when you pass the metal detectors. I'm quite sure that there are more of 'em spread throughout the place. Put it this way, if you ain't got the ratchet on you, ain't nuttin' poppin' off up in there without getting your neck damn near broke in the process." Hahmo informed.

When they pulled up to the entrance of the parking lot, Hahmo didn't even have to pull in and look around because Freaky's red, pimped out Lincoln LS was sitting right there in the first parking spot, on front street.

"Pull across the street. I'ma be out here, somewhere. As soon as that nigga comes out and walks toward his car, I'ma repaint his shit with some real metallic."

Hahmo parked the Durango, left his heat with his man and walked up to the door with his twin brother by his side.

"How's it going, fellas?" One of the bouncers tried to be friendly.

"Better, once we get inside." K.I. answered.

Once inside they were patted down and escorted to the bar by an Amazon thing that looked like a taller version of Gabrielle Union. Shorty would've been a vic on a thirsty night but the twins were strictly business looking for a tall Flavor Flav looking dude. He was supposed to be wearing a big name plate around his neck that read 'Freaky', in script letters.

The duo split up. Hahmo walked to his right and was to hit up the right side of the bar and the upper level, while K.I. was supposed to do the same on the left side of the club. The twins met up in the rear of the bar near the Champagne room and ordered two shots of Henny. A second later, Freaky exited the restroom area on the left and initiated the first part of the game, *hide and seek*.

Hahmo kept tabs on Freaky while K.I. described what was going down over the phone to B.R. After about two hours of waiting and lap dances, Freaky stood up and put on his Burberry rain jacket. Hahmo looked at his watch. 3:15 a.m. Freaky walked over and whispered something into the ear of a Spanish chick with a bubble ass, long blonde hair and a pair of irregular shaped titties. The airhead smiled and told Freaky that she'd be right back. When mami returned, she had a Dior overnight bag slung over her shoulder and followed Freaky toward the exit.

"Here he comes now, Blood. Burgundy Burberry jumpoff, with a big booty Spanish thing in his pockets. You need us to do anything?" K.I. offered.

"Leave two minutes after he does and pull the truck into position. I'ma get this over with as quick as possible."

"Two minutes it is."

Freaky exited the building and handed the bouncer to his left something that B.R. couldn't see. The blonde thing on his arm was giggling, probably from being tipsy and kept placing her hand into Freaky's jeans. When Freaky bent the corner and entered the parking lot, he noticed a car next to his with the hood open.

I hope this nigga don't need a jump start, he wondered.

As he got closer, something didn't seem right. The dude under the hood didn't have any light on illuminating the area to assist him with his mechanics. Freaky got as close as he could and tried his best to see what was up. "Yo! Yo, partner! Was' up?"

B.R. stepped from under the hood with a sawed off shotgun in his hands and a mask covering his grill. "Run, nigga and I'll open you up from your ass to your ankles." B.R. yanked Freaky by his hood and told the Spanish chick that was with him, "Sit yo' monkey ass on the floor and slide in between both of these cars."

Gloria did as she was told and found a seat between Freaky's Lincoln and the car that was parked next to it. B.R. grabbed Freaky and pushed his back up against the side of the LS. He raised the pump to Freaky's face and said, "Open ya' mouth!" Freaky complied thinking that it would save him, and Black Rose pushed the rifle about an inch past his lips. "Member me, homie?"

Freaky stared into B.R.'s green eyes, and when it all came back to him, with the gun still in his mouth, he managed a weak, "Let's talk about ...".

BLOOOM!

That's all she wrote.

B.R. kicked Miss Bimbo in the head, walked over to the SUV, got in and said, "Take me home, Blood. I'm done."

Hahmo took B.R. straight to his crib, dumped the stolen Jeep and hopped in the Impala they had parked outside of the Pathmark parking lot on a side block.

"You trying to go fuck something?" Hahmo checked to see if his brother wanted to get his freak on after a long night of drama.

"Who do you have in mind?"

"Patricia."

"You think she's with it?"

"Only one way to find out." Hahmo jumped on the Bronx River Expressway and headed south to 450.

Chapter Twenty-Nine

B.R. entered his home, stopped in the living room and just looked around at the immaculate set up. It had been a while since he could actually relax, due to all of the functions, business and beef he had been taking care of. He admired what Amiaya had done to the place and was thankful for having her in his life. He walked up to the second level of his home where he and Amiaya slept and peeked into the bedroom. Amiaya was sound asleep in the bed with the T.V. on. Jaime Fox and T.I. were talking about all the homies they lost and as B.R. stripped down to his birthday suit, he too began reminiscing about his dead homie, B.G.

He stepped into the shower, turned on the water and finally, after everything that he'd been through, knew that he was done with the streets. After a thorough cleansing, B.R. dried off, walked into the room where Amiaya was sleeping comfortably and slid into the bed next to her.

Mmtwa! He kissed her on the lips. Amiaya stirred a little but didn't wake up, so B.R. kissed her again. "Hey baby." She spoke groggily.

"I missed you, ma." B.R. expressed to her.

"I missed you too. You okay?" She stretched.

"Yeah, I'm good."

"Did you take care of what you talked to me about, earlier?" Amiaya had her hands all over her man's face and chest. She cared so much for her fiancé. She only hoped that he was done running around and ready for what she had to tell him.

"It's over boo. O'l boy will never rape anybody else, ever again. And the nigga that smacked you and took the Beemer, let's just say that him and the rapist are probably fighting for a cool place in hell right now."

"You sure you're okay?" She kissed his lips and rubbed her hands gently over her tummy.

"Positive."

"Are you ready for some good news?" She sat up on one elbow and smiled.

"I've been waiting all of my life to hear something good."

"I'm seven weeks."

"Seven weeks what?" He leaned up with her.

"Pregnant."

It took a moment to sink in but when it did, B.R. smiled and said, "Damn, I love you girl."

Amiaya threw her tongue into B.R.'s mouth and responded, "I love you, too." She guided him into her world and B.R. went hard because he was happy that he could finally live without his past being a burden on him. His past, according to him, is what led him to the streets. Now it was all behind him and he was ready to move on.

"What did she say when you told her that you and I were together?" K.I. asked Hahmo. Hahmo had called Patricia and was telling her how much he missed her. He reminded her how good her pussy was and asked her could he come through and get some more of her gushy right then.

"Where you at?" She had asked him.

"I'm pulling up in front of the building."

"Do me a favor, bring me up a gallon of milk, a big box of Apple Jacks cereal and a loaf of wheat bread."

"Is that all you need?"

"And that lovely thing that you have in between your legs." She laughed that statement out because she was getting excited just talking to him.

"You gon' get that, all day. But guess what?"

"What?"

"I got a surprise for you."

"What is it?"

"Two me's."

"Two you's?"

"Yeah, me and my brother."

Patricia remained quiet because although it was her fantasy to fuck two dudes at the same time, and had already been intimate with K.I., she didn't want them to think she was a slut.

"Patty." Hahmo called out.

"Yeah?"

"Check it, just be easy. We gon' smoke a few blunts, drink a lil Mo' and some Henny, and see where the mood takes us. If you start to feel uncomfortable, let me know and I'll tell K.I. to leave. You cool with that?"

"I guess."

"You still want the groceries, right?"

"Mm Hmm."

"Ahight. I'll see you in a minute."

Hahmo hung up the phone with a smile on his face so K.I. asked him. "What did she say when you told her that you and I were together?"

"She said we'll have to see when we get up there. First I have to grab up some food for her and cop us some Phillies and condoms. Do you want anything?"

"Nah, I'm good." K.I. declined Hahmo's offer.

"So meet me up there. Warm that thing up for your big brother." Hahmo cheesed. Hahmo only had K.I. by like 5 minutes.

"Ahight."

Hahmo and K.I. connected their hands together and threw up the Blood sign. "Eastside."

"All the time." Hahmo answered and allowed K.I. to head toward the building.

Hahmo walked into the store, bumped into a chick named Jennifer that he was trying to fuck and started talking to her.

When K.I. entered 450, he pressed for the elevator and the door opened up. He got in, pressed 4 and right before the door closed, somebody yelled, "Yo, hold the elevator!"

K.I. hit the button to open the door and a gentleman slid in but didn't press a floor. He said something crazy to K.I. that Killer only heard in the movie *Menace to Society*. As soon as the door closed, shots went off in the elevator. *Blocka! Blocka! Blocka!*

Hahmo heard the clapping and ran back to the building. A crowd had formed near the lobby so he had to push past everyone to get a good look at the dude on the floor. "Damn, somebody just shot crack head Darnell. Oh well, time to get me some ass." He said and hit the staircase.

Upstairs K.I. was heated. "Fuck he mean can he suck my dick." He mumbled just as Patty was emerging from the rear of her apartment in nothing but a pair of lace stockings.

The End

Fan Mail

contact

Antoine "Inch" Thomas
at

inchthomas@hotmail.com

or at

Amiaya Entertainment, LLC
P.O. Box 1275
New York, NY 10159

Attention

Urban Fiction writers abroad. If you're looking for an editor or Book DR., contact Antoine "Inch" Thomas at:

Amiaya Entertainment, LLC
P.O. Box 1275
New York, New York 10159
inchthomas@hotmail.com

Note: Antoine Thomas has edited over 50 manuscripts, check the entire Amiaya Entertainment roster.@ www.amiayaentertainment.com

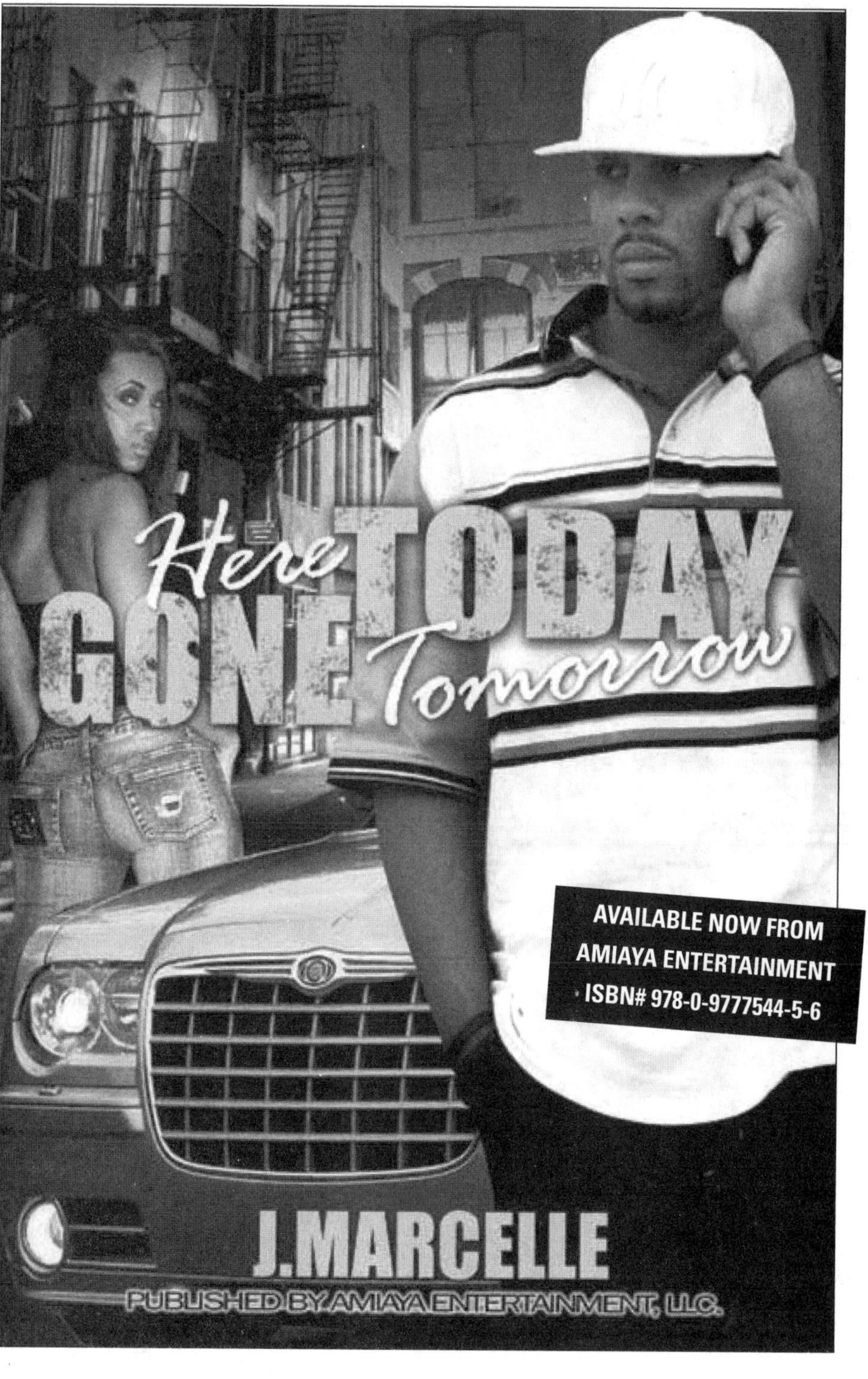

Here TODAY
GONE Tomorrow
AVAILABLE NOW FROM
AMIAYA ENTERTAINMENT
ISBN# 978-0-9777544-5-6
J.MARCELLE
PUBLISHED BY AMIAYA ENTERTAINMENT, LLC.

CHARLES THREAT

WINDOW
SHOPPER

PUBLISHED BY AMIAYA ENTERTAINMENT, LLC.

THE TRUE TO LIFE DYNAMICS OF THE "HOOD."

STREET
Khama

DWAYNE JONES

PUBLISHED BY AMIAYA ENTERTAINMENT, LLC.

Flower's Bed
The Most Controversial Book Of This Era

Written By

Antoine "Inch" Thomas

Suspenseful...Fastpaced...Richly Textured
PUBLISHED BY AMIAYA ENTERTAINMENT

From the Underground Bestseller "Flower's Bed"
Author Antoine "Inch" Thomas delivers you

NO REGRETS

It's Time To Get It Popping

"Gritty....Realistic Conflicts....Intensely Eerie"
Published by Amiaya Entertainment

"If It Ain't Rough, It Ain't Right"

THAT GANGSTA SH!T

Featuring Antoine "INCH" Thomas

Shocking...Horrific...
You'll Be To Scared To Put It Down
Published By Amiaya Entertainment LLC

A Diamond
IN THE ROUGH

JAMES "I-GOD" MORRIS
PUBLISHED BY AMIAYA ENTERTAINMENT, LLC.

ALL OR NOTHING

MICHAEL WHITBY

PUBLISHED BY AMIAYA ENTERTAINMENT, LLC.

HOE-ZETTA
VINCENT WARREN BRINGS YOU ANOTHER "HOT" NOVEL FROM AMIAYA ENTERTAINMENT
AVAILABLE NOW FROM
AMIAYA ENTERTAINMENT
ISBN# 0-9745075-8-X
VINCENT "V.I." WARREN
PUBLISHED BY AMIAYA ENTERTAINMENT, LLC.

So Many Tears

AVAILABLE NOW FROM
AMIAYA ENTERTAINMENT
ISBN# 0-9745075-9-8

Teresa Aviles

PUBLISHED BY AMIAYA ENTERTAINMENT, LLC.

A WOMAN'S WILL TO SUCCEED FROM THE LOW'S OF THE GHETTO TO THE TOP OF THE GAME

AVAILABLE NOW FROM
AMIAYA ENTERTAINMENT
ISBN# 0-9777544-0-5

A ROSE Among THORNS

JIMMY DA SAINT
PUBLISHED BY AMIAYA ENTERTAINMENT, LLC.

AVAILABLE NOW FROM
AMIAYA ENTERTAINMENT
ISBN# 0-9777544-3-X

Phone

Sister

—T. Benson Glover takes you
on a journey to the Badlands...

T. BENSON GLOVER

PUBLISHED BY AMIAYA ENTERTAINMENT, LLC.

"THEY DONT THUG NI#&AS OUT LIKE WE DO"

AVAILABLE NOW FROM
AMIAYA ENTERTAINMENT
ISBN# 0-9777544-1-3

THAT
GANGSTA
SH!T VOL. II

Featuring Antoine "INCH" Thomas

HERE COMES THE PAIN

PUBLISHED BY AMIAYA ENTERTAINMENT, LLC.

STORIES FROM AND INSPIRED BY THE STREETS

SOCIAL
SECURITY

IN THE HOOD WE TAKE CARE OF OUR OWN

PARENTAL
ADVISORY
EXPLICIT CONTENT

Will Truth learn before it's too late that all that glitters is not gold?

Truth Hurts

PUBLISHED BY AMIAYA ENTERTAINMENT, LLC.

SHALYA "SHAY" CRAPE

Flower's Bed the Sequel —Black Roses
ORDER FORM

		Number of Copies
Flower's Bed the Sequel	ISBN# 978-0-9777544-8-0	$15.00/Copy____
Window Shopper	ISBN# 978-0-9777544-6-4	$15.00/Copy____
Street Karma	ISBN# 978-0-9777544-7-2	$15.00/Copy____
Here Today Gone Tomorrow	ISBN# 978-0-9777544-5-6	$15.00/Copy____
Social Security	ISBN# 0-9777544-4-8	$15.00/Copy____
Sister	ISBN# 0-9777544-3-X	$15.00/Copy____
A Rose Among Thorns	ISBN# 0-9777544-0-5	$15.00/Copy____
That Gangsta Sh!t Vol. II	ISBN# 0-9777544-1-3	$15.00/Copy____
So Many Tears	ISBN# 0-9745075-9-8	$15.00/Copy____
Hoe-Zetta	ISBN# 0-9745075-8-X	$15.00/Copy____
All or Nothing	ISBN# 0-9745075-7-1	$15.00/Copy____
Against The Gain	ISBN# 0-9745075-6-3	$15.00/Copy____
I Ain't Mad At Ya	ISBN# 0-9745075-5-5	$15.00/Copy____
A Diamond In The Rough	ISBN# 0-9745075-4-7	$15.00/Copy____
Flower's Bed	ISBN# 0-9745075-0-4	$15.00/Copy____
That Gangsta Sh!t	ISBN# 0-9745075-3-9	$15.00/Copy____
No Regrets	ISBN# 0-9745075-1-2	$15.00/Copy____
Unwilling To Suffer	ISBN# 0-9745075-2-0	$15.00/Copy____

PRIORITY POSTAGE (4-6 DAYS US MAIL): Add $4.95

Accepted form of Payments: Institutional Checks or Money Orders

(All Postal rates are subject to change.)

Please check with your local Post Office for change of rate and schedules.

Please Provide Us With Your Mailing Information:

Billing Address_____ Shipping Address

Name: _____ Name:_____

Address:_____ Address:_____

Suite/Apartment#: _____ Suite/Apartment#:_____

City:_____ City:_____

Zip Code:_____ Zip Code:_____

(Federal & State Prisoners, Please include your Inmate Registration Number)

Send Checks or Money Orders to:
AMIAYA ENTERTAINMENT
P.O.BOX 1275
NEW YORK, NY 10159
1 646-331-3258

AMIAYA MAGAZINE

FIRST EDITION

The Entertainment Manual For Readers And Authors Alike

AMIAYA
ENTERTAINMENT

H.N.I.C.
ANTOINE "INCH" THOMAS

BROOKLYN'S
FINEST
JAMES "I-GOD" MORRIS

ALLENTOWN'S
2ND STREET
AUTHOR
MICHAEL "MIKEY RAW" WHITBY

THE BRONX
BOROUGH'S
OWN BAD GUY
VINCENT "V.I." WARREN

ICH IS IN
THE BUR
JIMMY DA SAINT

MAR 06

BEHIND EVERY GOOD
MAN IS A GOOD WOMAN
TANIA L. NUNEZ-THOMAS
CO-CEO AMIAYA ENTERTAINMENT

NEW HAVEN'S HEAVY HITTER
TRAVIS "UNIQUE" STEVENS

THE CITY OF BROTHERLY
LOVE'S
1ST ROUND DRAFT PICK
G.B. JOHNSON

AMIAYA'S 1ST LADY
TERESA AVILES

AND MUCH, MUCH MORE

PUBLISHED BY AMIAYA
ENTERTAINMENT, LLC

*with us,
it is what it is...*

Support the Soul Quest Records **MelSoulTree Project** by ordering your CD TODAY!

MelSoulTree's "Mel-Soul-Tree" **CD ALBUM**/ISBN# 8-3710109095-7 *$16.98*/Per CD_____
10 Songs + 2 Remixes
*** *SPECIAL "MAIL ORDER" PROMOTION* ***
FREE "FIRST CLASS" SHIPPING **ANYWHERE** IN THE UNITED STATES.
FREE Autographed POSTER when you buy **2 or MORE** MelSoulTree CD Albums.

Hurry! This FREE Poster Promotion is available while supplies last!!!
Please allow 7 Days for delivery. Accepted forms of payment: Checks or Money Orders.

CREDIT CARD ORDERS can be placed via www.CDBaby.com/MelSoulTree2
OR
Call CD Baby at: **1 (800) Buy-My-CD**
NOTE: Credit Card Orders <u>will be</u> charged $16.98 + S&H. Credit Card orders are NOT eligible
for the FREE poster offer.

Please provide us with your BILLING & SHIPPING information:

| BILLING ADDRESS |

Name:_____

Address:_____

Suite/Apt.:_____

City: _____ State: _____ Zip Code: _____

| SHIPPING ADDRESS |

Name:_____

Address:_____

Suite/Apt.:_____

City: _____ State: _____ Zip Code: _____

If you are ordering 2 or MORE CD's... Please list the name(s) that should be signed on the FREE
autographed poster. _____
Send Checks or Money Orders <u>along with this form</u> to:

Soul Quest Records
244 Fifth Avenue, Suite K210
New York, NY 10001-7604
www.MelSoulTree.com

We thank you in advance for your support of the Soul Quest Records MelSoulTree Project. www.MelSoulTree.com

Melissa Thomas, born and raised in the New York City Borough of the Bronx is both beautiful and talented! **MEL-SOUL-TREE** (Melissa Rooted In Soul), a sensational R&B soul singer (with a strong background in Gospel music) is signed to the international **Soul Quest Record Label**. This vocalist has been described as having "an **AMAZING** voice that is **EMOTIONALLY CHARGED** to deliver the goods through her **INCREDIBLE** vocal range."

MelSoulTree can sing!! (Log on to www.Soundclick.com/MelSoulTree to hear music excerpts and view her video "Rain" from her self-titled debut **CD**). **MelSoulTree** has performed worldwide. She has established musical ties in France, Germany, Switzerland, Argentina, Uruguay, Chile, Canada and throughout the U.S.

LIVE PERFORMANCES?
MelSoulTree's love for performing in front of live audiences has earned her a loyal fan base. This extraordinary artist is blessed, not only as a soloist, but has proven that she can sing with the best of them. **MelSoulTree's** rich vocals are a mixture of **R&B, Hip Hop, Gospel and Jazz** styles. This songbird has been blessed with the gift of song. "Everyone speaks the same language when it comes to music, and every time I perform on stage, I realize how blessed I am."

PERFORMANCE HISTORY
MelSoulTree has worked with music legends such as: **Sheila Jordan, Ron Carter, The Duke Ellington Orchestra, The Princeton Jazz Orchestra & Ensemble, Smokey Robinson, Mickey Stevenson, Grand Master Flash** and the **Glory Gospel Singers** to name a few. This sensational vocalist has also recorded for the **Select, Wild Pitch, Audio Quest, Giant/Warner, Lo Key** and **2 Positive** record labels. She tours internationally both as a soloist and as a member of the legendary **Crystals (a group made popular in the 1960's by Phil Spector's "Wall of Sound")**. **MelSoulTree** is known affectionately as the "Kid" or "Baby" by music legends on the veteran circuit. "Working with the **Crystals** has afforded me priceless experience, both on stage and in the wings being 'schooled' by other legendary acts while on these tours." According to **MelSoulTree**, "performing and studying the live shows of veteran acts is the most effective way to learn to engage an audience and keep my performance chops on point at the same time."

MUSICAL INFLUENCES
Minnie Riperton, Phyllis Hyman, Stevie Wonder, Marvin Gaye, Chaka Khan, Natalie Cole, Rachelle Farrell, CeeCee Winans, Ella Fitzgerald, Whitney Houston, Alicia Keys, Mariah Carey, Yolanda Adams and many others... "A lot can be learned from new school and old school artists... good music is good music! I want to be remembered for bringing people **GREAT** music and entertainment!!

FOR MelSoulTree INFO, CD's & MP3 DOWNLOADS VISIT:
www.MelSoulTree.com , www.Itunes.com & www.TowerRecords.com
For booking information please contact **Granted Entertainment at: (212) 560-7117**.